Silent Dreams

CARRIGAN RICHARDS

Silent Dreams
A January Dreams Novel
By Carrigan Richards

Cover design by C.R. Graphics.
Edited by Lindsey Alexander.
www.readinglisteditorial.com
Proofread by The Literary Vixen

To learn more about author Carrigan Richards, visit her
website at www.carriganrichards.com

Also by Carrigan Richards
Standalone Novel
Pieces of Me

Elemental Enchanters Series
Under a Blood Moon
Under the Burning Stars
When Darkness Fell
Under the Winter Sun
Under an Onyx Sky

January Dreams Series
January Dreams
Silent Dreams

ACKNOWLEDGMENTS

I had gone through something personal that took over everything. I couldn't write. I couldn't read. Listening to music was just there. It wasn't until I started telling my family and friends what was going on. I felt better, but I still couldn't write. I tried forcing it, but you can't do that. It was like there was a wall that prevented me from truly getting back to myself. After months of hardships and obstacles, I finally climbed that wall, but I wasn't over it. I just kinda stayed there because it was a relief to have made it that far. I never thought I would finish this book. Words would come, but I couldn't concentrate on it. I spent so much time fretting about if I had any words left in me. Turns out, I did, and still do. But I had to get over that wall. And once I finally did, BAM! The words flowed out of me. I had to let myself heal before I could come back to my characters and the worlds. I am forever grateful to those who helped me through all of the heartache, depression, insecurities, and much more.

Thank you to all my fans who have stuck by me no matter what. You are truly remarkable.

Angie, you have been nothing short of amazing. Your kindness, patience, and friendship has meant a lot to me, and I don't know where I'd be without you!

Laura, you have been an amazing friend and supporter. I can't thank you enough for all your hard work, for keeping me in line, for cheering me on, for helping through the tough times. You always know how to help a girl out when she's down. You have a beautiful soul. I love you, boo!

Jennifer your unconditional love and friendship through all the years has never gone unnoticed.

Nicole thank you for being my writing buddy and for

listening to my vents and for helping me through it.

Sarah, I can never thank you enough for your kindness and for always being so supportive.

Gina, you are a rock star. I don't know how you do it, but you are truly super woman.

Stephanie thank you for all your advice and laughter.

Christal – I can't thank you enough for your help!! I love you, my friend!

To the newest bunch of amazing ladies I've met this year: The Sweetness Crew. Jimmy Eat World brought us together, and I'm so happy we met. Thank you for all of the support, ears, and love. And of course, Jimmy stalking.

To all the musicians who continue to pour their hearts out that helps get me through the hardest times of my life, especially to Jimmy Eat World. Your song, "You Are Free" lifted me out of one the darkest times.

To my mom and Rob; my dad; Morgan and Alison. Carla. Thank you for your support and for cheering me on. I love all of you.

Patrick, you are the best brother a girl could ask for. Thank you for believing in me, for the awesome book talks, and for keeping me company on the drive home.

To Brandon – for being patient and caring and loving. Thank you for your never-ending support and encouraging me every day to get these words written. You inspire me and I admire your strength. Thank you for believing in me and my dream. You are incredible.

For Laura, who helped me get my creative juices flowing
and who never gave up on me.

Do not let your fire go out, spark by irreplaceable spark in the hopeless swamps of the not-quite, the not-yet, and the not-at-all. Do not let the hero in your soul perish in lonely frustration for the life you deserved and have never been able to reach. The world you desire can be won. It exists. . . it is real. . . it is possible. . . it's yours.

—Ayn Rand, Atlas Shrugged

Prologue

Whoever said that everything happens in slow motion right before you die, is right. That's what it was like for me. Fleeing for my life, running as fast as I can, right into Casper Truitt's arms, finally. Many lifetimes ago, he and I met a witch who gave us a potion to drink. A special serum that allowed us to live as humans and be reborn after each lifetime. We would spend each human life searching for each other unknowingly, until our hearts inevitably found their way to each other, and the memories would return.

None of the lives were as dramatic as this one. The one where Vincent found us and tried killing both of us. But I escaped, leaving him to die in the burning house. I ran all the way to Casper's home. He'd pulled into the driveway, his car still running, his lights shining on us.

It's May, but it's cold outside that it feels like October.

Casper jumps out of his car and rushes up to me.

"Casper—" His lips cut me off. Soft, warm, and eager. We finally found each other. I lose myself in his kiss, forgetting, if only for a moment, being held captive and knowing Vincent's confessions. Casper is all I need, and I want him forever. I love him, and I don't care what anyone thinks.

But we can't keep running.

"Casper," I say as he rests his forehead against mine. His hands rake through my hair, which feels matted. "We can't keep doing this. We have to get the Jewel. Vincent followed us, and he'll do it again. I know he has the Jewel. He has to. It's the only way he's here."

"I know. What happened? Where have you been the last few days?"

"Vincent drugged me. Locked me up in his basement. I set it on fire and left him."

"Is he—"

Dead. "I don't know. I just ran. Everything came back to me. All the memories. Everything about us. I had to get out of there."

He takes a deep breath and kisses my forehead. He tilts my chin up. "Everything's okay. I promise. I love you." Casper fans my hair out from my shoulders and his fingers brush against my neck, sending a hot shiver up my spine. I can't tear myself away from his brown eyes and I inhale as he leans down, pressing his warm lips to mine. The same rush fills me like in my dreams. There is nothing else but us. I press my body to his, wanting him closer as our mouths slip over each other's. My heart can't be tamed. It's like a wild horse who has escaped, freely running.

A loud crack sounds, though it doesn't distract me enough to pull away from Casper. His lips are on mine kissing me as though it's been years since our last. It feels that long, and I've missed him. But the blinding white pain that suddenly washes over me, forces my body to go slack. Casper holds me to keep me from falling.

"Megan," Casper cries.

The agony swallows me. Burning, searing throbbing. I take short, shallow breaths.

"Hold on, Megan!" His voice is muffled by the pierce ringing in my ears. My eyes are heavy, and my body is numbing. I can still hear his voice and I cling onto it with everything I have. But I'm fading. The pain is too much, and I can't hold on. "I need help. Please. She's...shot!"

I see the fear in his eyes and feel the gentle way he caresses my face. I want to touch him, but I can't move.

His words jumble in my mind as my eyes close.

Slowly, slowly, I hear no other sounds.

ain erupts throughout me. I can't open my eyes. Or move. In all my human lives, I never died so violently. I don't know what happened. Sounded like a gun, but I can't be certain. Panic grips me. I know I'm dying.

But after a few moments, the pain vanishes. Just like Casper's voice.

The ache is replaced by some weird vacuum feeling. It's as if something is dragging my body through the air. Maybe it's a tornado whisking me away. It sounds like a wind tunnel, and it scares me. Nausea roils inside my stomach. Is this what it's like to die? If it is, it's definitely not what I expected.

It's quiet now. No wind tunnel, no nauseous feeling. Nothing. Warmth and serenity settle over me. If only Casper were here with me.

"Megan!" I hear him screaming for me, but I still can't open my eyes. It's like a bad dream that I can't force myself awake.

Panic sets in. Bathing me in layers and layers of unease. Men shout from afar. Constant gunfire pops in the distance. Deafening explosions shake the earth and I feel their vibrations inside me. I hear the screams of people; the fear in their cries fills the air. It's hot. So hot, it feels like I'm next to fire. When I feel a breeze, I catch a hint of salty ocean air.

Where am I?

Wake up.

I need to get out of this.

Someone roughly lifts me into their arms, jostling me like they're running. It makes me feel sick and I need to be on my feet. I need to steady myself. Moaning, I try to release myself from this tight grip.

"Megan, wake up!" I hear his voice. I want to see his face. "Come on, Megan. You have to wake up." He shakes me, not hard, but enough to open my eyes.

I gasp when I see Vincent's dark blue eyes. They're urgent, and fear settles in them. A sickening feeling clutches my stomach and I struggle to get out of his arms. I drop to the ground, landing on soft sand.

No.

I can't catch my breath as I scan my surroundings. There are cliffs on my left side and a fire engulfed forest on my right. Vincent stands before me. I have to get away from him. He shot me. Locked me up in a basement.

Where am I?

This feels too real. My dreams always felt real. This is a dream. It's just another dream.

I'm so groggy. Or Vincent found a way inside my head again. This isn't real. I found Casper and someone shot me. I'm unconscious, that's all. I need to wake up. "Get out of my head. I need to wake up."

"Megan." Vincent looks down at me like I'm the most pitiful being, then he looks around in a panic.

Something whistles in the air. Seconds later an explosion rumbles the ground. Debris crashes near us, scattering sand everywhere. Cowering, I scream.

Vincent seizes my arm, jerking me to my feet. "We've gotta go. We're in the middle of the damn warzone."

I have to force myself awake.

I shake my head, but it's no use. He pulls me away from the fire and the earsplitting sounds of bombs and guns and terror. As we run, I glance down and see that I'm still wearing my white prom dress. Although, it's hardly white anymore with all the black soot, blood, and dirt. I reach around to my back to where, I swear, I was shot, but there isn't a wound. Just wet blood.

Casper. Where is Casper? I pull against Vincent's hand. "Where is Casper?"

"Not here."

No matter how hard I struggle against him, he wins. My heart sinks. After all my efforts to get away from him have failed, I realize I can never escape Vincent. I don't know Casper's fate, but I don't want to think of him as anything but alive.

I tug my hand from Vincent again and he halts pulling me to him. He holds that old familiar sultry look in his eyes. It used to bring me to my knees, but now I fear him. I know what he's capable of and I know how naïve I have been. A wave of terror washes over me.

"Stop fighting me," he says sternly. "I have to save you. We have to get out of here."

I shake my head. "Save me? You shot me. You tried to kill me."

"*You* tried to kill me, Megan. I didn't shoot you. By the time I found you, you were unconscious. I brought you back home to *save* you. Now come on!" He tightens his grip on my wrist and drags me along.

Back home? "You mean we're…" My voice trails as I look around once more. The cliffs. The familiar landscape of the dark, green forest across from the vast ocean.

Vincent has brought me home to Arvada where a war still rages on. I'm no longer in the human world and I am once again running in order to live.

Two

"How could you do this to me?" As I wipe the tears from my cheeks, the sand roughly scratches my face.

It's been several miles, my legs are exhausted, and I'm out of breath. I don't know how long we ran but we followed the shore until we got far enough away from the sounds. The orange sun peeks out from the horizon, and I collapse in the cool, brown sand as Vincent finally releases my wrist. It aches from his tight grip and it's raw.

In the last twenty-four or however many hours, I went from escaping Vincent, finding Casper, getting shot, to being ripped away, yet again from Casper. Vincent has taken me to Arvada. I can't help the tears that stream down my face. That was the reason for the weird vortex I felt. Vincent used the Nuummite Jewel to teleport us home.

If Casper dies in that lifetime, he will be reborn and never find me. I have no way to return without the Jewel. Unless I find the witch.

"How could you *shoot* me?"

Vincent turns with his hands on his hips, breathing hard. His eyes soften. "Megan, I didn't shoot you. I can't believe you would even think that. I would never hurt you."

Guilt collects at the base of my throat, but I let the anger push it down. I clench my fists. "You *drugged* me! And locked me up. What is wrong with you? Why did you follow me to the human world?"

"I can explain everything."

"Why did you bring me back here?" My chin quivers and the words catch in my throat. Knowing Vincent brought me back without Casper terrifies me.

"Hey." He kneels in front of me, taking my shoulders in his hands. "It's okay, Megan. Take a deep breath. I know all of this is scary, but I promise you I will get you home safe and out of all this."

I push him away. I don't want him touching me. "Tell me what happened."

"By the time I reached you, the shooter was gone. You were dying, Megan," he says, his eyes watering. "I had to do the only thing I could to save you. I brought you home. Where you healed."

"Save me? I was fine! Even if I had died, I would've come back. But you knew that, and you still brought me back because you can't stand the thought of me loving someone else."

He shakes his head. "He manipulated you to get to me. He only wanted the Jewel. You're right about one thing. I can't stand the thought of you loving such a horrible creature."

I let out a frustrated snarl. "Casper isn't the bad guy. He's treated me better than you ever did."

He flinches. "All of it was a lie. He never loved you. He let me take you home."

"What did you do to him?"

He pinches the bridge of his nose. "Nothing, okay?"

"Why did you bring me back?"

"You were attacked and then someone shot you. Someone obviously wants you dead. Yes, I kidnapped you, but it was only to bring you back here where you can be safe."

"Are you joking? We're in the middle of a warzone."

"I have no control over where the Jewel takes me. If they killed you in the human world, they could've brought you back here and killed you for good."

The truth of his words sends through my veins.

"Megan, you were never safe with Casper. He sent someone after you again." The muscle in his jaw twitches.

"Again?"

"Megan," he says my name like a warning.

"What is it? Tell me."

"He sent Adam after you."

I let out a sigh. "Whatever. Do you get off on all these lies?"

"You used to trust me. That revolting Elf has been feeding your mind with nonsense."

I groan. The lies keep piling up with Vincent. Why did I ever believe him? Clenching my teeth, I want to strangle him. "No. *You're* the one feeding my mind with nonsense. No one's coming after me. Least of all, Casper."

There's a hardness to his eyes and it scares me. I don't want to be afraid of him anymore. I want to be free of him. Of this manipulation. This control.

He shakes his head. "Your mind is so messed up that you don't even know what's real anymore."

I can't argue with that.

Vincent gets to his feet, peering out into the ocean. It's beautiful and as the sun sinks further into the water, it brings on a chill in the air. I can hear the waves pounding the cliffs.

"When are you going to open your eyes and believe me?" he asks, his voice hoarse. "Casper convinced you to leave with him. And you followed along like some lost little puppy."

Rage fills me. "Why would he spend lifetime after lifetime with me as a human if all he wanted was the Jewel?"

"That's the thing about Elves. They are patient, calculating creatures."

I shake my head. "You are so full of it. Why would you even say that?"

"Because it's the truth. I only tell you the truth, Megan."

I laugh. "Why not give him the Jewel? It belongs to the Elves anyway."

"I did."

That brings me up short. "What?"

"I gave him the Jewel so I could have you back. I told you. He didn't want you. Once he got it, he disappeared, leaving you."

My heart clenches. *No.* Casper would never do that. He loves me. "You would never give up the Jewel."

A mixture of defeat and sadness flash across his eyes. "I did. For you."

Whatever.

Scrambling to my feet, I get in his face. "You think after all this, I'm going to forget him and fall in love with you again? You can't keep erasing my memories, Vincent."

A muscle in his jaw twitches. "You begged me to erase them last time. I would never hurt you. Yes, I tried killing Casper because I was protecting you. He's dangerous, Megan. Yes, I drugged you and locked you up because I had to bring us back here. You are under a spell and I'm trying to save you."

I slap him across the face. "You didn't have to do that. You could've told me."

"You are *compelled.* You wouldn't have listened. I had to do it."

Tears sting my eyes and as I raise my hand to slap him again, he grabs it. A vision overcomes me. It's Casper. Holding me but I'm unconscious because I'd just gotten shot. Vincent rushes toward him.

"What happened?" Vincent cries.

"She was shot," Casper says. "Like I told you would happen because my first warning wasn't enough."

"What warning?"

"Adam." He gloats.

"You son of a bitch." Vincent moves toward him, but he holds me back.

"The Jewel, Vincent. If you don't give it to me, I'll keep living and dying with her. Over and over. Making her mine. Using her. She'll never want you again."

Vincent clenches his jaw. "I'll give it to you as soon as we get back to Arvada."

"You know she's not dead. She'll die in this life, but she'll be reborn. Looking for me. Always me." Casper's lips stretch into a menacing grin, and he juts out his chin.

Vincent removes the Jewel from his neck and slowly hands it to him.

Casper reaches for it, dropping me to the ground. Then, the vortex starts.

I squirm out of Vincent's hands. "What was that?"

"Dammit! I didn't want you to see that."

"What was that?"

"*That* is what happened, Megan. He doesn't care about you."

"You only show me what you want me to see," I say, but I know that isn't true.

He frowns. "I only show you the truth. You know I can't make up a vision. I never wanted you to see that."

Casper would never give me up like that. He'll come for me. It was a ruse.

Wasn't it?

As I stare out into the ocean, the waters are as uneasy as my stomach. It feels like the air has been knocked out of me. It was never real. Casper never loved me. He sent Adam to attack me. He used me. A tear falls from my eye and I swat at it. I don't want to cry for him.

Even though we're far enough away, I can still hear the pops of gunfire and booms from bombs. The sounds of men shouting and guns nearby. My breath hitches as I look in the direction of the chaos.

"Come on. Let's go," Vincent says.

"I'm not going with you."

He snatches my sore wrist. "Megan, please believe me. I would never hurt you or let anyone hurt you again."

"I can find my way," I say, bravely.

"You can fight them off?"

"I'll tell them who I am, and Casper will come for me."

He gives me a pointed look. "They will kill you. You're a Sprite. He'd be the first to tell them how he tricked you only so he could steal the Jewel back. Come on."

Somewhere deep down inside, I know he's right. No way would the Elves believe me.

But has Casper been playing me all this time? How could I have fallen for it? All this time it was Vincent who has been on my side.

As the pain tugs at my heart, wanting to know the truth, I leave with Vincent.

Three

A rush of cold air fills the night. I can't tell if the loud sounds are from the waves hammering on top of each other or if it's explosions and gunfire. The way the tree branches reach out makes it look like some monster trying to grab me. I long to fall asleep in a warm bed, away from this cold and desolate place.

I wish I weren't wearing a freaking prom dress. My shoeless feet ache and bleed. If Casper were here, he would make sure I had proper attire for running.

But he wouldn't be here. Because some stupid Jewel is more important to him. Am I that dumb? What is wrong with me?

This is the longest nightmare I've ever had. It needs to end.

I try so hard to be brave and not think about how much I miss him, or even my human life. I miss Cherry. Our long talks on the phone or hating being at work. My parents and Jonathan. Staying up late, watching a movie with my big brother. I'd even rather be arguing with Ron than deal with this. I miss sitting in my room listening to music and writing. Spending time with my dogs. What I would give to cuddle with Savannah in bed. I took it all for granted. Somewhere deep down inside, I knew something like this would happen.

But I'm home now. Where I belong.

Vincent and I come upon an abandoned castle that is now mostly ruins. Ivy covers the blackened stone walls, or the few walls that are left.

The inside feels empty. Pieces of jewelry lay cracked on the ground as some are melted together. Black and gray ashes are scattered across the floor of broken picture frames and lost mementos from the family who once lived here.

I find a quiet corner and draw my knees to my chest. The bottoms of my feet are bloody, and they throb and sting. I don't care. I can't let myself get lost because Casper never cared. No matter how much my heart breaks, I can't lose myself to all the mind games. It's up to me to save myself and I know I'm strong enough. Casper reminded me of how strong I am.

Until he gave me up for the Jewel.

Gazing into the sky through the open ceiling, I want to find Casper. Find out if he only wanted the Jewel. I can find him through our dreams.

I shake my head. I saw the vision. They are always absolute. The emotional part of me refuses to believe Casper would give me up but the logical part of me knows he betrayed me. Why would he do that to me? Why would he spend life after life with me? Vincent was right. They are cold, calculating creatures.

Curling my knees up to my chest, I rest my head on them.

"I'm sorry," Vincent says as he sits on the other side of the room from me. His voice is hoarse, and he looks exhausted.

My heart sinks. He never apologizes and by the looks of it, he means it. "Why?"

"I know none of this is easy for you."

"Who shot me?"

"I don't know. I'm guessing another Elf."

I don't understand how he still cares for me after everything I've put him through. "Why do you even want to be with me after all I've done?"

"Because I love you. None of this is your fault. I blame myself. If I had only been there more. If I had done more. The King was hellbent on war and it made me lose you in the worse possible way."

"Why haven't you tried erasing my mind?"

He shakes his head. "I'm not doing that again. You have to find your own way and make your own decision. I'll bring you home, but you have to decide."

I look up, meeting his eyes. "What?"

"Megan, no more games. Casper messed with you. *I* messed with you, trying to protect you. No matter what you choose, I will always protect you and I will always choose you. But I can't force you to love me."

Well, this is certainly a change of events. I wonder if it's all more games to him. So much has happened. So many lies and deceit. Doesn't anyone actually love me? Have I been a pawn in a chess game this whole time?

"Why haven't you been able to let me go? Is it some obsession? Can't stand to see me without you? I mean, your hatred for the Elves is deep. Even before Casper came along and it can't be because of your father."

"Because they are our enemy. Same reason you should hate them. You see what they're capable of. You saw the vision. Elves are not innocent people. Now that they have the Jewel, they will try to compel every single Sprite into believing their way of life."

"If they could do that, they would've done it already."

"What's to say they haven't? You grew up hating them as much as I did, yet all of a sudden after meeting one, you believed in them. You wanted to give up everything, including your Sprite life."

"You're wrong." Except, he's not. Casper compelled me into loving him. "How do I know you didn't do the same to me?"

"I don't have the same powers as the rest of the Elves."

I look up at him and freeze. His ocean blue eyes pin to mine with desire that I once craved. "What?"

"Nothing." He turns away.

"What did you say, Vincent?" My heart is beating against my chest.

He tosses his head back, then meets my gaze. "I love you, Megan. I wish I knew what was so different about me that you left me so easily. We were to marry. You and me. It was always you and me. Until you met *him*. What was so special about *him*? He's an Elf and so am I. You fell in love with two Elves."

Four

"Stop lying," I yell.

He shakes his head and gets to his feet. "I'm not lying, Megan. Why do you accuse me all the time?"

I've seen that dark, crazed look in his eyes before. When he found Casper and me in a cottage together. He shot him leaving him for dead. But what if Vincent was saving me all those times? No, he's not perfect, but if he is an Elf, he only loves one person. It definitely explains his fierce protection.

"You want to know why I've hated the Elves my entire life." He clenches his fists. "I hate them because my mother abandoned me."

"What?" My stomach twists. This can't be true. "How are you an Elf? You show no markings of one.

Your father is a very powerful Sprite. Why on earth would he care for an Elf baby?"

"He and my mother had an affair. Things went sour and once she gave birth to me, she left me. Left me for dead. She wanted the ocean to swallow up her mistake and move on like it never happened. But my father found me and saved me."

"What?" My heart sinks. "Vincent?"

"Who does that to their own child? No matter how much she hated him, she didn't have to try to kill me. I have nothing but contempt for the Elves."

"That's impossible. There has never been children of Sprites and Elves."

"It's all been kept a secret."

"Why didn't you ever tell me?" I'm hurt by this. Hasn't he ever trusted me?

"You never wanted to hear such things."

I get to my feet, facing him. "You never gave me the chance. You always keep everything to yourself. Of course, I always feel left out because you close yourself off. Why can't you ever open up to me?"

He drags his hands down his face, and frowns. "I wasn't allowed to say a word to anyone. This has been a secret that I've had to keep." Tears well in his eyes. "My *mother* wanted me dead. I was raised by Sprites, so I always thought of myself as one. When I found out, I was angry and in denial. I wanted to ignore it or act like it never happened. I don't want to think of myself as an Elf. Had I told you before, you would've exiled me."

"You don't know that."

He gives me a knowing look. "The only reason you're not repulsed by me is because you've been spellbound by an Elf. Even though Elf blood flows through me, I don't exactly possess the same powers as they do. I can't compel you to love me. My love for you is real."

"Will I always love him? I mean, is there any way to end the spell?"

"I don't know. Maybe we can track him down and force him."

I don't understand though. Legends of our kind have been telling the same story for centuries. The Sprites and Elves are at war with each other because of a stolen Jewel. A Jewel that I learned the Sprites stole from the Elves in order to kill their kind, since the removal of the Jewel essentially makes Elves mortal by speeding their aging until they eventually die.

Is that even true? Have we been lied to this entire time?

"If the Elves knew one of their own possessed the Jewel, there would be no war. Why didn't you tell them the truth?"

"They don't know who I am. For all they know, I never existed to them. The Jewel is mine. It was created for me once I was born. Sure, I gave it to Casper, but I have every intention of getting it back. I *have* to have it."

"Why?"

He meets my gaze. "I'll die without it. The Elves cursed me and for all their lives, they've been told some ridiculous story of the Jewel, hence the war."

The curse is the cause of the war and I let an Elf in my head and my heart making things worse.

My head spins from everything I've learned in the past several hours. I keep thinking any minute, I'll wake up, warm in my bed and Savannah slowly creeping out from under the covers. My phone dinging with a text from Cherry.

But this is real. This is my real life and I've got to do something about it.

Casper never loved me. A pain in my chest stabs me at the thought. Vincent has never left my side; and everything he's done for me was to save me.

If Vincent needs the Jewel back, we can work together on getting it. Find Casper and end the spell. Or find the witch to end it. I can't believe how misguided I've been. How easily manipulated I was. I still love Casper and I hate that. He made me hate Vincent, and I've loved Vincent my entire life. We were so in love and I have to remember it. We never had any issues until Casper came along.

"What if I help you get it back?" I ask him.

"What?" He studies me carefully. "You believe me?"

"Yes. I'm not the best person and I've not treated you well. Especially since Casper. The Elves are the enemy," I say as a bulge builds in my throat and tears threaten to escape.

Vincent lets out a long sigh. "We should get some rest. We have a long day tomorrow."

Hugging my knees tighter, I lean my head against the cold brick wall, gazing at the beautiful stars. If I could only reach Casper. To ask him why he did this to me. How he could've done this.

A dark cloud approaches. Fast. And it's not from the lazy wind. The cloud appears to have wings. I rise to my feet and my heart races.

I rub my eyes, knowing I need sleep as it's been several hours since I've gotten any. I swear I see a dark cloud with wings floating above silently. It flaps its wings like a heartbeat as it blocks the moonlight. And then...it's gone. My heart drops to my stomach. What did I see? Wings? I'm losing my mind.

"Vincent." I look over to the other corner but he's not there. Instead, he's running toward me.

"We need to leave, Megan," he says and grabs my hand.

"Did-did I just see—"

"The Dragon? Yes. The Elves are looking for us. Come on."

Five

When I was a little girl, my father used to tell me stories about dragons. One in particular. The legendary dragon. It was the one who kept the Nuummite Jewel. Both Sprites and Elves believed the other controlled the dragon. Legend says he flies only at night, like a nightmare drifting in the sky, waiting to pounce on the innocent. I haven't thought about a dragon in years. Once when I was a little older, I thought I saw the dragon, but my father just chuckled. I realized what a silly children's story it was that my father told me.

As Vincent and I tear through the forest, I know for a fact I did see a dragon, and again, seconds ago.

The forest is large, gloomy, and primal. Its canopy is marked by evergreens, poplar, white ash. I can barely see where we're going but I clutch onto Vincent's hand, grateful he can navigate through the thick branches. I'm running on a mixture of sand and pebbles and wet, slimy things and I'm so tired of running. I'm so tired of being afraid.

This isn't happening. They don't exist. It's only a legend. Vincent is messing with my mind, yet again. He's playing on my exhaustion. He has to be. I shake my head. That's Casper's voice in my head.

As soon as Vincent finds a small hut along the beach, we seek solace. The thunderous waves crash on top of each other. The wind is colder here and as it rustles through the leaves on the trees, I panic thinking it's the dragon.

We sit, panting, wary of the dragon. Quietly waiting for any sign of it.

I shiver, hating that I'm still wearing this stupid dress. I want warmth. My heart is still pounding from running, and from everything I've learned in the last few hours. I'm tired, my feet are blistered and bleeding, and my heart and mind are struggling.

"What is happening? This isn't the same place that I remember," I say looking around at the barren land.

"A lot has changed, Megan. Jacques is king now and he's trying to right this situation."

"Your father?"

"King Jacques," he corrects.

How did Vincent's father become king? He isn't exactly deserving of the crown. He deserted men on the battlefield. He's killed innocent people. Did

Vincent convince the entire Sprite population to agree with that? What has happened?

"None of this is real. The war. Dragons." I can't breathe. I want the dream to end already.

"Megan." He takes my hands in his. "It's okay."

I shake my head. "No. I saw a cloud that looked like a dragon."

"I'm sorry. It's real. You've spent much of your life living in some fantasy world. This is real. This is our life. Dragons exist."

I take a deep breath. "I want to go home. When are we getting there?"

"I know. I'm trying to get us there as fast as I can."

I sink to the ground and curl up. How far can I get if I run? I don't know where to go. Rancid scents float toward the sea, mixing with the salty air. It smells like death, at least what I suspect death smells like. The bleakness of it all will forever haunt me.

I can't run. Not yet. I need to rest. I'm so exhausted. My eyes are heavy and my body is worn out.

One reason I was able to run with Casper all those years was because we took care of each other. We worked well together.

A tear escapes my eye. I miss him. I ache for him and it's driving me crazy. It hurts being away from him. I hate the pain that clusters inside me. I take a deep breath, calming myself. I am stronger than I think I am. I can get out of this.

Stupid Casper. He has to get out of my head. I hate how messed up my mind is.

"Why haven't I ever seen a dragon before?" I ask, my voice hoarse and tired.

Vincent frowns. "Because I erased every single memory you had of them."

"Why? Were they bad?"

"They always terrified you, and I hated that."

I want to remember everything. No matter how awful. It's a part of me. Who am I without my memories?

I hate that I let someone remove my memories or to even mess with my mind. Brainwashing is apparently a specialty of Casper's and I let him take full advantage of it with me. I let him take over and even in my human life. How could I do that? Am I that weak? Naïve?

Vincent begins to strengthen the makeshift shelter, while I gather firewood. Once I find enough, I start a fire, remembering all the times Casper and I made a fire. The warmth it provides calms me and feels amazing.

I wonder about my human family and Cherry. What do they think happened to me? Do they think I disappeared? No one knows I was shot.

Sadness bears down on me, and I try not to fall down the rabbit hole. I can't help but think of all the memories of Casper and me.

I glance at Vincent standing in the water, waist-high, with an improvised spear, trying to fish. It's too dark and there is no moon sparkling across the ocean. It seemed to have taken hours for him to catch a fish and when he did, he brought it over to the fire.

The night is quiet, no signs of the dragon. But I still can't sleep. Before Casper and I realized who we were, I dreamed each night of our life together. It didn't make sense at the time but those are my memories. Now, I have no dreams.

In one of mine and Casper's human lives, we met as kids. I didn't have the best home life and he always took me into a field, pretending we were in a faraway world. Captains on a ship. Fantasy land riding on the back of a dragon. I never held a single fear when I was with Casper. He always gave me strength, in every life we shared. I knew I could face my worst fears or any problem no matter how hard, as long as Casper was at my side, and he always was. He never let me down.

Feeling the sharp ache in my heart makes me want to give up. I feel empty without him. Not knowing if he's alive or dead leaves the hole in my heart greater. But he gave up on me. After all of our lives. I was nothing to him.

No matter what, I will survive this, no matter what hell I have to go through. I will prevail. I wipe the tears from my eyes.

"For what it's worth, I'm sorry for what he did to you. I hate him for what he did."

"Why didn't you kill him?"

His eyes narrow. "What?"

"After all he did. And now he has the Jewel. Why didn't you kill him?"

"I was more concerned with saving you. You deserve better than that. He was never right, and I know I'm not the best. But I will do anything to make it up to you. We deserve our own happy ending."

"Yeah. You're right," I say like I'm a robot. Going through the motions but the feelings aren't there. I don't know what I feel. Leaning against the cold rock, trying to hold myself together, I close my eyes. I don't want to sleep. Not with Vincent so close by and not with some mysterious, mythical dragon flying around. My eyes betray me, and my shivering body wakes me.

"Here," Vincent says and when I open my eyes, I flinch. He's inches closer with his arms open.

I take a deep breath and curl myself into his arms. I thought it would make me want to crawl out of my skin, but I don't feel anything.

"We should find him and get the Jewel back," I say. "He should pay for what he's done."

The entrance of Village Féerique has tall metal doors with guards standing on both sides in red uniforms. Looming at the top of the hill is Château de Fées in all its beauty. I can barely make out the intricate metal lattice atop the palace.

The guards open the gates, and we enter the village. I never expected to feel so emotional returning home. Growing up, I used to visit the village to the shops and the people. They were always so welcoming and kind.

But as we walk inside the village, a heavy putrid stench hits me and I'm not sure what it is. I swat at congregating flies that seemingly multiply. A lot of the villagers look sickly and thin. It's obvious King Jacques is neglecting them. But why? Does he not think they are deserving? How did he even become king? Did Vincent persuade the previous King to hand over the reins? Why would he do that? He's never had a stellar relationship with his father.

We continue through the village, and everything is different from what I remember. The homes and shops are in terrible shape. Holes in roofs. Porches falling apart. Men and women are wearing dirty clothes. It's as if the village has no money at all.

It was never like this. I can't remember the last time I walked through here. There is a lot of commotion in the center of the village as Vincent tows me through the heavy crowd. People angrily shout but they aren't focused on me. Their attention is on the stage up ahead. I can barely see. Too many tall people, but I look up and see a man with a hooded mask on the stage, like the ones we saw in old movies that involved hangings and such. Executioners.

"What's going on?"

"Beheadings," Vincent replies and keeps moving.

My heart stops. *Beheadings?* Since when did the Sprites ever execute anyone? Are they killing Elves?

Vincent doesn't release my hand and it's hard to follow with all the pushing and shoving. Heat pours over me, and I can't breathe. I almost feel like we're at a concert or something. I've never seen the square like this. The pounding beneath my chest doesn't stop. My stomach churns with a sickness and I hate the anxiety that consumes me, making me shake. I need to get out of this.

"Keep moving, Megan." He double backs and practically shoves me through the crowd, not before I hear the blade slam down on the wood.

I feel sick.

Some people celebrate with joy while others scream in horror. I don't think I'll ever forget that sound.

Gasping, I turn around, but Vincent blocks my view. "You don't want to see this."

Once we reach the outer edge of the village, I stop, haunch over like I'm going to throw up. "What did they do? Why are there so many?" I saw more than five people on the stage.

"Because they committed crimes."

We were never so hostile toward our own kind. What has changed?

We climb the path toward the gates of the palace. I'm exhausted. Heartbroken. Confused. Lost. Guards nod toward Vincent and open the gates. Once they open, we start walking down the long gravel path. The small pebbles stab my feet, so I move to the grass. It's much calmer here, and part of me relaxes because this is my home.

The beautiful well-kept garden is laid out in an ornamental labyrinth of low hedges and fragrant, colorful flowers. Gorgeous, massive trees are scattered alongside the edges of the palace grounds. I used to run through here with Vincent. We were so happy here. Even as a small child, I played here with Florence. I miss her and being home isn't the same without her. But Vincent's men killed her for escaping with the Elves. It makes me wonder why I was spared, and she wasn't.

The palace has clearly stood the test of time, the rocks of the walls are aged, and vines and plants grow inside the cracks. The baroque architecture is breathtaking, and I didn't realize how much I would miss it. This hasn't been my home in years. At least, it feels that way. Time here moves much slower than the human world. It's only been seven years since I've been gone, and the castle hasn't changed. At least, as far as appearances. It stands wide and while three stories are visible, its lower levels are underground. Its brick and stone are all white and the flat roof is grey. A dome accentuates the center, while two turrets decorate the left and right sides.

This is where I met Florence as kids and we played too close to the water, or ran too far in the fields, or rode our horses too late. It's where I fell in love with Vincent.

And met Casper.

An ache squeezes my heart.

Guards open the double ornate doors, and we enter, my breath catches in my throat. The ceilings are adorned with illustrations of Roman gods. The walls are cluttered with paintings of soldiers and kings accented with gold. There are several of King Jacques portraying gods and I see J's intertwined throughout almost as a reminder that he is *the* king. It's almost like I'm seeing it for the first time.

I forgot how beautiful and grand the palace is. The limestone floor is cold against my feet. My tattered dress is far too out of place. Vincent covers my shoulders with a blanket.

"We must see my father, then I promise you, we'll get to our rooms and clean. Are you okay?"

Sure. I just saw several people get murdered and walked by like it was nothing. "I'm fine. Let's get this over with."

"I know."

He squeezes my hand and takes me to the throne room. We stop at the edge of the room as two men in guards clothing duel each other with their swords. A drunken audience stands on both sides of the fight, cheering.

The throne room is vast and grand, with a prominent crystal chandelier hanging from the center of the room that has gold accents. The crown molding is all in gold and has a complex design. A scarlet rug runs down from the throne and marks the closest spot people can stand when they address the king. Swallowtail banners with ornate needlework drape from the walls. Between each banner hangs a lit torch, illuminating the sculptures of kings and legends below them. Broad, stained glass windows depicting divine beings are edged by veils colored the same scarlet as the banners. The curtains have been adorned with embellished borders and emblazoned edges.

At the head of the room, watching the men fight, is King Jacques in a sublime throne of brass. He's completely engaged in the fight, in front of a crimson curtain that hangs from the canopy. The throne is covered in gilded crests and fixed on each of the wide armrests is a lavish demon wing.

The cling and clang of the dueling soldiers brings me from my reverie making me jump. I'm appalled. Since when does the king request duels? Especially in the throne room.

The man with red hair stabs the other. My breath hitches.

The injured man groans, his eyes roll back into his head, and he collapses.

It's disgusting what Jacques has done. Turned the Sprites into animals. He doesn't care what happens.

Vincent grips my hand and holds me close to his body.

Jacques claps as he gets to his feet. "Lord Nicolas, you can't be defeated," he slaps his shoulder. "Get this body cleaned up."

Two men nearby rush to pick up the dead man's body. Like it's nothing but trash.

"Vincent, my boy!" He welcomes Vincent with a hug and when he sees me, his blue eyes light up. Jacques stands tall, and while he may appear old, he's not at all frail. Deep scars from the many wars he has fought are embedded into his pale skin. The black king's robe he dons covers his large, hulking body. Gold outlines his outfit and a matching crown rests on his short white hair. I spent so many decades in the human world, I've almost forgotten what it's like to be a Sprite.

I am supposed to curtsy? How can I curtsy to him? My legs refuse to move.

Vincent clears his throat, and my knees decide to cooperate. I bow before King Jacques, feeling disgusted with myself.

Jacques approaches me and takes my hand in his. "Lady Megan, I am glad that you're back. Those Elves won't get away with it."

"It is good to see you, my King."

"I know Vincent is happy you've returned."

"As am I."

His eyes rove over me like I'm a dessert buffet. I hug the blanket tighter around me. "I suspect you will need to clean up."

Vincent wraps his arm around me, and I feel the tension between him and his father. "We're on our way now. I wanted to let you know we've returned."

"I trust you took care of a certain problem?"

"I did. It's done."

I can only guess he's talking about Casper. He didn't mention that Casper stole the Jewel. For good reason, too. Jacques wouldn't be happy.

"Wonderful. Perhaps this calls for a celebration."

My stomach churns at what his idea of a celebration would be. It definitely won't be a masquerade ball. Or anything remotely civil.

"Sure." Vincent nods. "We'll discuss in the morning."

"Very well. Lord Nicolas, let's see who else you can defeat."

Men drunkenly cheer as Vincent ushers me out of the throne room. I can tell he's frustrated by the hurried way he walks and the clenched jaw.

As we climb the familiar spiraling staircase, we pass the windows that show the golden wheat field swaying under the dusk light. The field reaches for miles over rolling hills. My heart sinks as I remember speaking to Florence in that field.

Vincent leads me up through another hallway with slender braziers at the bottoms of each of the obsidian columns. The flames shroud the hallway in a dark orange radiance. He opens a mahogany door, and we enter a vast bedroom with long burgundy velvet curtains and a canopy bed with sheer matching red drapes. The furniture is all mahogany, and all of my little trinkets are still here. After all this time, nothing has changed. It's like Vincent preserved the room for me.

My fingers brush over a brass heart-shaped box. Vincent gave it to me many years ago.

"I never touched anything," Vincent says. "I wanted you to have your room just as you like it."

"Unlike the rest of the castle," I mutter under my breath.

"I'm sorry you had to see that. Things aren't the same here."

"It shouldn't have even happened. How long has this been going on?"

"A while now. You'd know if you'd been here."

His comment stings a bit and I turn to him. "Vincent, even if I never met Casper, I don't think I was very happy here. I never felt like I belonged."

"What are you talking about? You belong here."

I bite my lip. What I saw today were hellions, clearly out for blood. If I can't keep up the charade of being kidnapped, what will they do to me? Am I safe at all? "After what I've done, no one likes me. I am an enemy to them."

"You have to prove that you are one of us."

"How? As the only Sprite who has been taken by the Elves multiple times and hasn't been punished? As the only

Sprite without powers?"

"You aren't the only one."

"No? Who else?" I ask, challenging him.

He takes my hand in his. The soft look in his eyes used to send funny, warm feelings throughout me, but I feel nothing. Rather, I don't know what to feel. Everything here is different now. Nothing looks the same, and I feel a weird emptiness everywhere.

"Megan, this is your home."

"It *was* my home. What happened? Why are the homes in the village falling apart? Why were several men getting beheaded in the gallows earlier? Everyone looks poor, as if there is no money. And your father—"

"The King," he corrects.

"The King. What was he doing in the throne room? If he's the king of the Sprites, what is he doing? He's not preparing them for anything."

His jaw twitches. "The men in the gallows were traitors. They tried to assassinate the King. The homes are falling apart because those same traitors decided to let them get that way. They were too busy preparing for a ludicrous plan. They have plenty of ways to make money. They choose not to. Unfortunately, for the display downstairs, that was Jacques being drunk."

I shake my head. "If people have revolted against him, don't you think that's a bad sign?"

"You haven't been here. You haven't seen all the good he's done."

Crossing my arms in front of my chest, I challenge him. "What good? Why do you always defend him?"

"Megan, it's late. Can we talk about this tomorrow?"

"How did he even become king? What happened to the previous king?"

"He died. In his will, he stated for Jacques to become

the next leader. Don't read too much into this. He is our King."

It's déjà vu. Everything. The story I have to tell people to convince them I was kidnapped by the Elves again. How many times are they going to believe it?

"How many times have you brought me back?"

"I've lost count," he says.

"Why does it keep happening? Why do I feel so out of place?"

Vincent rubs the bridge of his nose. "Because of how Casper made you feel. What he made you feel. One day, you will remember the truth. I know all of this is confusing but you have to set aside whatever Casper made you think and feel, especially when you are around others. No one can know you are still under his spell. If they do, they will hang you for treason."

I swallow hard, knowing he's right. I let out a sigh feeling the exhaustion take over. There is still a part of me that hopes once I fall asleep, I'll wake up in the human world. I return my focus on the accessories on the vanity. The silver brush set. Everything is so modern in the mortal world. There isn't even a hair straightener. No phone. No radio. Just the noises in my head. Which is more muffled silence. "They won't keep believing the same story."

Vincent moves behind me so close I can feel his breath on my neck. "Then make it convincing. You've gotten so good at lying. Casper made sure of that. You have to push him from your mind."

I grit my teeth but let go of the pressure. I turn around and search his eyes.

Vincent sighs, and sadness creeps into his dark blue eyes. "I hate seeing you like this and there isn't anything I can do. Yet."

"I never meant to hurt you."

"I know. Look, we both need to rest. Tomorrow, we can start over. I know it will take time, and I will do whatever I can to help you." He moves a strand of hair from my face. "We will get through this. Goodnight mon trésor. I will see you in the morning." He kisses my forehead.

I see a vision of us together from the past. We're happily playing chase in the gardens. He catches me and I giggle, loving the way his arms wrap around me. Loving the passionate kiss he gives me. I miss that happiness.

"I miss that," I tell him.

"I know. It'll come back. Julienne will be here in the morning."

"Who?"

"Your lady in waiting."

I give a small laugh. "Could've used one of those in the human world."

"Get some rest."

Sighing internally, I nod, watching him leave the room. I hear the unmistakable sounds of him locking the door on the outside, though I'm not sure if that's to keep me from running away or to keep the bandits running around this place from entering.

I let the blanket fall from my shoulders, and peer at myself in the mirror. All I see is a sad, worn down girl. Her black hair is matted beyond repair. Blood, tears, and dirt cover her pale skin.

I'm beyond eager to change out of this disgusting, tattered prom dress. It doesn't even look like the sweet, beautiful white dress I bought. Soot and dirt have blackened it. Blood has stained it. I remember the first time Casper saw me in it. The fervent look in his eyes stole my breath, and we danced with such ease, as if we had been partners for years. I can still feel the gentle way his fingers intertwined with mine as we moved across the floor. It felt like we were the only two people in the world.

The dress is all I have left from the human life. The last one I will ever have with Casper. The last one I found happiness.

I sigh, annoyed. Why can't I stop thinking about him?

Tears pool in my eyes but I push them away. I can't weep. I must stay strong. I cannot be weak. They will see right through me. I must be a Sprite. Play the part. Vincent wants me to blend in. Then so be it. I will live the life. I will be who he wants. I will forget Casper and his spell. I have to.

What I wouldn't give to call Cherry and get her advice. I can't stay here. I wasn't lying when I told Vincent I didn't belong here. In the mortal world, I belonged. I felt at home. It felt right.

I shake my head. Those are thoughts of a scared little girl. We'll get the Jewel back and end the spell. We'll get our revenge.

Seven

Rolling onto my side in bed, I stare at the curtains blocking the morning sunlight. No dreams came to me. Against everything inside me, I cried myself to sleep. Whether Casper's love was real or not, it's no longer there. None of it. I wish I could stop dwelling on it. No matter how much someone hurt you, it's still hard to forget them or erase them and all the memories from your mind. I thought of ways to get the Jewel, but nothing came to mind.

I can't give up.

The room is lonely. I miss waking up to Savannah burrowing her way out of the covers, or Cherry texting me. Or even my mom yelling at me to turn off the alarm clock. I smile at the memories. As mundane as my human life was, it seemed to have purpose and I miss it. I long to get back to it. Something feels wrong here, and I don't know what it is.

I take a deep breath. Things will get better once we fix it. I'm not even sure how much time Vincent has.

There is a quick knock on my door, then an unlocking sound. A tall girl with a round face and tight brown curls enters. Her skin is as porcelain as mine and her dark eyes are sad. She looks worn-down, almost as exhausted as I looked last night.

"Good morning, Lady Megan." She curtsies but doesn't make eye contact.

"Are you Julienne?"

"Yes, ma'am."

"Oh please, you don't have to call me that." Pulling myself out of bed, I wince once my feet touch the floor. They are sore and blistered. All of my muscles are tight, and everything hurts.

Julienne silently helps put some sort of ointment on my feet and helps me with a corset. It's awkward having someone help me dress and I don't like it. As soon as she finishes tying every knot for the corset, I want to scream out so many obscenities. The damn thing hurts and cuts off my breathing. Whose bright idea was it to wear these stupid things?

I ease myself into a white cotton dress with ruffles and winged sleeves. I long to wear leggings and a shirt. Julienne gathers my long black hair and ties it, letting it rest against my nape.

"Are you okay?" I ask her.

"I am fine, ma'am," she says, but I don't miss the hint of resentment? Annoyance?

Another knock on my door and Julienne answers it, curtsying when she sees Vincent. When he enters, I hold back a laugh as he's dressed in brown pants that come to his knees with white stockings. It's been ages since I've seen him in such clothing.

"Good day Lady Megan. Your Royal Highness." With that, she leaves the room, closing the door.

"Is she okay?" I ask him.

He shrugs. "Why?"

"I don't know. She seemed like she was pissed at me."

"Want me to find out?"

I shake my head. "You look ridiculous."

He laughs. "Can't say I miss this wardrobe."

"I can barely breathe."

"Well, for what it's worth, you look beautiful," he says, and I know he means it.

"Thank you. You look handsome, my Prince."

He rolls his eyes. "It's a little strange being back here after so long. One day, we can introduce them to a newer wardrobe. Did you sleep okay?"

I shrug. "I'm sure it'll take time to get used to everything."

He nods. "Yeah. The mortal world is definitely more advanced."

I chuckle a little. "Just a bit. I miss having a cell phone."

It's so easy to fall into a conversation with him. I remember how easy it was for us. We always fell in sync, though I'm not sure what caused him to be so dark in our human life. Maybe it was finally finding me and having to deal with Casper.

He moves aside. "Ready?"

"Vincent, how much time do you have? I mean, should we be wasting it on visiting my parents?"

"We'll be fine. I promise." He lifts his elbow inviting me to take it and when I do, we leave.

I haven't been in the castle in what feels like centuries, and it hasn't changed. The stares are the same. The Sprite girl who was kidnapped by Elves numerous times and who had her memories erased. I don't even know how many times it's been. Would my own people try to hang me? The way Vincent's father has these people brainwashed I wouldn't put it past them. Would Vincent let that happen? The sheer and nonsensical violence that occurred last night has me crawling out of my skin.

It's uncomfortable walking through these halls. Vincent and I make our way outside to a horse-drawn carriage.

That sense of not belonging edges its way inside me, but something else is there. Like a cloud of darkness hovering over me. Paranoid, I look into the bright blue sky searching for a dragon. When I don't see one, I climb into the carriage with Vincent.

Clutching onto the seat, we make our way to my parents' estate in the horse and carriage. As I peer out the window, the steady clip clop sound of the horse's hooves calms me. The beautiful French countryside passes us by. Wildflowers stretch beyond the horizon, meeting snow-capped mountains. It seems almost surreal to see while there is a war happening not far from here.

The last time I saw my parents was at a party at the castle. Since being engaged with Vincent, I moved to the palace and tried to see them as much as I could.

It's only been seven years to them, but it's been centuries for me since their only child ran away with an Elf.

"Do they hate me?" I ask.

Vincent frowns. "No, of course not. Why would they?"

"Because of what I did."

"You can't be so hard on yourself. You were compelled."

"Erase the compulsion then. You're an Elf. Take it away."

"I tried that once and it didn't work. Besides, you don't want me to erase anything. Your mind has been through so much and I don't want to make it worse. It needs to rest."

No argument here.

The carriage comes to a stop in front of a two-story brick home. Eight windows surround the red door of the flat fronted house. There are no balconies or porches.

Dread and anxiety sink in at the thought of facing my parents. Vincent is right. I left my parents without a word. I don't want to lie to them, yet I can't tell the truth.

He takes my hand and squeezes. "Everything will be fine, I assure you. I will never leave your side. You are mine and I am yours, mon beau trésor. Never forget that."

I have no doubt that Vincent will be by my side from now on. Seeing as his father is now the leader and he no longer wishes to be part of the army. I have no doubt that he will keep me safe.

"Are you ready?" he asks.

I shake my head.

"They are eager to see you. It will be fine."

The driver opens the carriage door and holds out his hand for me. Placing my hand in his, I step out and onto the gravel road. Vincent emerges and takes my hand, forcing me to look at him. Pity shows in his dark blue eyes.

"Let's go." I attempt to pull away, but Vincent wraps his arms around me. A real hug.

"I have missed you," he says. "We're home now, together. As it was meant to be. We have all the time now."

Emotion overcomes me. I know I wasn't fair to Vincent in how I left him. He was never there, and I strayed. I wanted something more. Something to cure the emptiness inside me or the cruel ache. He wore me down and I wanted to be happy. I don't know if my seemingly sudden loss of interest is what made him lose it, or knowing I fell in love with an Elf. Or a combination of both. I never meant to hurt him, and it's hard to remember that since he's hurt me numerous times. We both hurt each other. We're both victims, yet it's my fault.

I draw back a bit and give him a smile.

He places his hands on the sides of my face and kisses my forehead. "Come on."

We walk inside the home and an elderly man leads us to the parlor.

A small frail-looking woman sits in a tall, backed chair, needlepointing by the window and my heart leaps. Her delicate hands work feverishly without mistake, like she always has. She's so concentrated on it she doesn't hear the butler announce our presence.

The second she looks up tears immediately cloud her blue eyes. She rushes up to me and pulls me into a hug. "Thank you, Vincent for returning her." She weeps and I feel a tug at my heart. I didn't want to hurt my parents. My father joins us and gives me a quick hug.

"Thank you," he tells Vincent.

"Did they hurt you?" Maman asks. "You've been held captive for so long this time."

"I'm fine, Maman." As she expresses such joy, I realize how good it feels to see them. How much I have missed them and the deep regret I feel for leaving them. In all my human lifetimes, I always thought of them.

"Always so strong," she says, cupping my chin and studying my face. "It's because of yours and Vincent's love. You held on so tight for him."

I smile.

She hugs me once more. "Please don't get captured again. Don't let them take her. My heart can't take it."

Her words are like the nail in the coffin. It will crush her if I leave again. Perhaps I can convince her to come with me, I know she would never last one day in the mortal world.

She takes me to a corner in the room where we can have some privacy, while Vincent and my father talk amongst themselves.

"I can't tell you how happy I am to see you, my child. Vincent always came back to inform us of your well-being. He explained everything. The witch, the potion, all of it."

"He came back?"

She nods. "He wanted to make sure we knew you were okay and that he had a plan to bring you back." She takes my hands in hers. "I know he is not perfect, and I know he had to do things to you that were extreme, but you must know he did it for us. I told him to do whatever it took to return you to us. He was so conflicted over so much of what he did, he has feared so much that you would hate him. Megan, you cannot hate him. He loves you with all his heart. He has a pure heart."

I don't know what to say or think. All of this was to bring me back to my parents. Glancing at him, I'm so overcome with emotion. I remember Casper always telling me to stay away from him; that he was dangerous, but he was fulfilling my parents' wishes. Casper threw me away for a Jewel. I understand Vincent's hatred for them.

How could I have been so blind? How could I have let Casper compel me? How could I have fallen in love with Casper?

"I know you and Vincent are staying at the palace, as it's expected since his father is King. You should know you both have a place here. I know his father has never treated Vincent as well as he should."

I nod. "Of course."

"Now, despite all the bad that happened in the mortal world, was anything good?"

I tell her about my dogs, Cherry, and how modern it is. She doesn't understand most of it, but she listens with a keen ear.

Vincent and I visit with my parents a while longer, catching up and making sure Maman is relieved.

On our return trip in the carriage, it's quiet again. Vincent and his father haven't always had the best relationship and I wonder if it's because he's part Elf. Jacques has never exactly been proud of Vincent, even for all that he's done, especially for his father. Vincent's always loved my parents, as they've held him in the highest regard. He's saved their daughter. He's fought in countless wars. He would do anything for them and me.

I can find his mother. Get her side of the story. Maybe I'm eager to end King Jacques's reign. Vincent's deep-rooted issues are because of Jacques. I could never convince Vincent to leave his father, but I wonder what kind of person he'd be without him. I don't want to be at the castle any more than I have to and if Vincent isn't there, perhaps he won't be swayed by anything King Jacques says to him.

"Vincent?"

"Hmm?"

"I want to see my parents every day."

He studies my face and after a few moments, I take his hand and intertwine my fingers with his.

"I shouldn't have left. I know that. It's my fault that all of this heartache and pain has happened. My parents." I swallow hard. "And you deserve much more than this. I need to see them. I need them to know that I'm home. For good."

Relief washes over his face as he squeezes my hand.

"Je t'aime ma chérie," I whisper as tears cloud my vision. "I'm so sorry for hurting you. I will do anything to prove that. We need to get the Jewel back."

"We will."

"They've caused too much pain. The Jewel is yours; it belongs to you. Let's go find it."

Vincent leans over, his lips inches from mine. "We will, mon trésor."

He kisses me, slow at first. It turns eager and I return his kiss. The heat and passion don't envelope me like it always did before. I don't know what is wrong with me. Except, I do. It's the spell.

"When can we start looking for it? I want this to end."

"Megan, you can't help."

"What? Why not?"

"It's too dangerous. I can't have you out there looking for it and risk getting kidnapped again. Or worse. I can't be out there searching for it and protecting you."

"What am I supposed to do?"

"Be patient and trust me."

I shake my head. "I can't stay there alone. Not without you."

"It'll be fine. I promise. I have everything taken care of."

He doesn't seem at all concerned. Does he have a plan in place that I don't know about? How does he plan on getting the Jewel? Is he even planning on getting it back? I don't understand his nonchalant demeanor. Maybe he still doesn't trust me. He thinks if I see Casper, I'll give up everything or have Vincent killed. I'm too much of a risk to do any good.

If he's going to do this himself, then I'll find the witch to end the spell. I refuse to be locked up in that palace with a psychotic king.

Eight

Grey clouds envelop the sky as I meander beyond the palace toward the village. I watched Vincent leave the palace and head toward the village. He can't know I'm gone and if I'm to find the witch, I have to be quick about it. Plus, if I'm going to stay here, I need to find out what happened to Château de Fées and the village. Why Jacques became King. Or how, rather. I tried getting information from Julienne this morning, but she told me not to ask such questions and kept saying how good the King is. It's a strange, robotic response that seems to be imprinted among everyone here.

As I pass through the village, the people stare at me with hatred so thick it penetrates through me. Do they know what happened to me? Can they tell I'm fighting a spell?

I always used to come to the village to visit and to shop, but it's not like that anymore. The heavy rotten stench is still there. There are drops of blood around the stage and ground from the other night. I refuse to investigate closer for fear I might see something that I don't want to see.

Lingering a way back, I see Vincent speaking to a man who looks like a blacksmith. A few minutes later, he leaves the village.

When I see a young woman holding a baby, I make my way toward her. "Bonjour madame."

Her face contorts into disgust. "L'ordure," she says. *Trash.*

"No, please. I-I just want to ask about the King."

She spits in my face and walks away, leaving me shocked. Does she think I'm trash for running away? How does she know? How am I supposed to convince people what happened?

Feeling several eyes on me, blood rushes to my cheeks as I wipe the spit from my face. Taking a deep breath, I continue through until I find a man working on horseshoes. I watch him shape metal into a perfect semi-circle. His calloused hands work mechanically, and I assume he's done this for many years. Dirt and grime cover his face and short blonde hair, but his green eyes are vibrant. When he glances up and sees me, he falters, almost hammering his thumb.

He bows before me, which makes me feel awkward. I don't think I'll ever get used to that. It's also strange that people, whom I've never met before, know me. "What can I help you with today, Lady

Megan?" His clothes are covered in dirt and tattered beyond repair. I can't recall a time any of the villagers wore such old clothing. They were always clean.

"I...I'm curious about things."

"Like what?"

"You're pretty!" A young girl appears from behind him. She has his green eyes, yet her blonde hair is curly and frazzled. Her innocent and exuberant smile is contagious.

"Thank you," I tell her.

"Are you from the palace? I hear it's pretty."

"You've never been?"

She shakes her head.

"Marie, that's enough." A woman with the same curly hair approaches and takes Marie's hand. "Lady Megan." She bows. The man continues hammering the metal.

"Are you here to purchase horseshoes?" the woman asks.

"I bet she has a pretty horse, Maman."

"I'm sure she has a lot of pretty things." The woman roves her eyes over me in a resentful manner and I feel heat rising to my cheeks. I feel ashamed of being here in my clean dress and the gold rope necklace Vincent insisted I wear. He gave it to me when we were younger, saying it was a symbol of our strength and that if I ever needed him, the rope was to represent him pulling me to safety.

"How come we don't?" Marie asks.

Her words knock the breath out of me. "Marie," the man warns. "Claudette, please take her home." He tells the woman.

I unclasp the necklace from around my neck and kneel before the girl. "I received this when I was your age from my—." I stop, not knowing what to call Vincent. "It is something to represent hope. If you ever catch yourself falling, grab the rope and it will catch your fall."

Marie's blue eyes light up and her jaw drops as she takes the necklace, but Claudette snatches it from her, handing it back to me. "We cannot accept this." Her eyes dart from side to side as if she's making sure no one is watching. Why is she paranoid? Are there guards in the village observing their every move? Did Vincent say something?

I frown. "It is a gift. I ask that you take it."

"Please, we cannot." She holds the necklace out for me, and I only take it because of the anxious look on her face.

"What did the prince talk to you about?"

"We cannot discuss that."

"What about the other night?"

"Came to gloat, I see." Anger crosses the man's eyes, and his demeanor turns cold. "Give us fancy gifts so you'll see if we turn against the King. We have nothing but the utmost respect for King Jacques."

"Jules, don't be so rude."

"No, that isn't it at all. I'm not here to gloat. I promise." I pause, hating what I'm about to say. "I have been held captive by the Elves for years and have just returned."

Studying me, he begins to soften the tiniest bit. "Sorry to hear that, but you cannot bribe us."

"That is not my intent. I only wish to know what has happened, as no one in the palace will tell me. H-how did Jacques become king?"

The man shakes his head and begins to hammer the horseshoe. "Lady Megan, perhaps there is a reason the palace will not tell you anything. You should not be asking such questions. Nor should you be here."

"What do you mean?"

"Your kind doesn't come near us."

What is he talking about? Marie mentioned that she'd never seen the palace. Has King Jacques revoked their right? What happened to the parties? The balls? "What do you mean? I don't understand."

"Palace folks do not mingle with the villagers," Claudette answers. "You really have been gone a while."

Since when did that take place? I also don't miss how no one seems to know the prince's fiancée had been missing. Didn't the King want to search for me? Didn't he want to help his son find me? "The King never visits you?"

"No, never. We do not visit the palace."

"Claudette," Jules warns again. "Take Marie home and stay there."

Claudette and Marie curtsy to me, then turn away from us.

"If you are fishing for answers, you have come to the wrong place. We have no qualms with the King."

"Please tell me something. I will leave you alone. Everything has changed and it isn't the same place I used to call home."

Jules lets out a long sigh. "Your being here is risking our lives. If the King sees us talking or suspects, I will be beheaded."

"That's senseless. Why would he do such a thing?"

"These are the times we live."

"Did the men from the other in the gallows revolt against the King?"

The cold look in Jules's eyes sends shivers down my spine. "Madame, I beg you to not ask me such questions. I have a family to care for and if I am dead, no one will."

Defeated, I nod, and begin to walk toward the gates of the village. I've spent too much time here and I have to find the witch. There is obvious hatred from the villagers toward the King and anyone who resides in the palace. It has nothing to do with what I did. No one will talk to me for fear they will die. How can Jacques do this? How is Vincent okay with all of this?

I reach the gates, but the guards block my way. "Excuse me, I say."

"No one is to leave," one of them says.

"What? Why?"

"Orders of the King."

You've *got* to be kidding me. What the hell is going on?

Shaking my head, I turn around. Once I get closer to the gates of the palace, I notice a rustling in the bushes. Someone whispers for me. "Lady Megan, please."

Glancing around to make sure no one sees me I walk into the bushes and crouch. Claudette is there. "My husband is only protecting all of us and I love him for it, but I see you are innocent and not privy to what has happened."

"Why did the men revolt against the King?"

She purses her lips. "Those men did not deserve that fate."

"What happened? Please. I must find out. I will not speak to anyone of this. You have my word."

"The King decided to use their wives for pleasure."

I gasp.

"On the lookout for a queen, I suppose. Ever since he became King, every single night, he summons a different woman to the palace. If he likes one, she will live there until he is through with her. Then he tosses her out in the cold as if she's nothing more than everyday garbage, forcing her to find her own way back home. They are used to his liking and none of them return the same. A few have even jumped off the cliff because of what he did to them. Their families disappear, too. No longer here."

Revulsion swarms over me and tears spring to my eyes. What have I come back to? "How devastating. I assume that if the husband or the wife decline—"

"Our home will be burned or worse, we will be beheaded. I tell you this because as someone as beautiful as you, you must watch out. Jacques doesn't care who you are. We have been severely cut off from everything. We are to work and provide the King with tools or whatever he needs, and he does not pay us much at all. It's barely enough to get by. The King always takes the best food and leaves us the trimmings and bad food. There are no doctors here."

"Why do you stay?"

"Lady Megan, forgive me but we've nowhere else to go. We are prisoners in our own home. Should we leave, we would only become prisoners by the Elves, as you know what that is like."

My heart drops. What a tyrant. How has no one fought back? Has he made it impossible to live? These people are tortured and hungry, while he stays in the comfort of the castle. I can't let this continue. I must do something. I have to come up with a way to end this. End King Jacques.

"The prince came to tell us that I am to go to the palace tonight. As the King's date."

No. I tense as my pulse speeds. I try to level my breathing. "I promise you that I will do whatever it takes to make this right."

Claudette shakes her head. "There is nothing anyone can do."

"You have my word."

She watches me quietly and nods.

"I will speak of this to no one. If you ever have any problems, come find me."

"How? We are not allowed in the palace."

"Leave me a signal or a message. I will check these bushes daily. We will get our home back."

I squeeze her hand and turn toward the palace.

I don't care why Jacques has completely cut off the villagers since becoming King. Whatever his reasons, it's not enough. No wonder why so many revolts against him. Why wouldn't they? Who would want to fight in his army? Though, looking at how controlling he is, it doesn't seem like anyone has much of a choice.

Even Vincent seemed uncomfortable around his father the night we returned. Something must change. My eyes focus on the castle, and while I must return, the thought makes my skin crawl. What if Jacques decides he wants to use me? Will Vincent have to comply? Will he fight against his father? Will he protect me like he promises?

My feet are heavy as I make my way back to the palace. The pounding in my chest is so loud that I can't hear anything else. Everything is muffled and I can't catch my breath. I stop against the palace wall and rest.

This is not my home anymore. It's not anyone's home.

That uneasy feeling returns. I can't live like this—no one can. I have to talk to Vincent. We have to end this.

The emotion is overwhelming, but I have to control it. No one can see me like this. Quickly wiping the tears, I take a deep breath and walk inside the castle. I am not afraid.

No matter what, Jacques won't get away with this. I will make sure of it.

Nine

I pace my room like some crazed woman. Everything Claudette said replays in my mind like some scary story I read as a child.

Except, this is real. *Ugh.*

The corset is cutting off my air. I remove my dress and the corset. Once it's off, I take a deep breath. My chest aches from it. Even if the spell lifts, how can I live like this? While people are being tortured and others turn a blind eye.

I have to pretend like I don't know anything. At least, during dinner. They acted so afraid to speak to me and I worry that I may have done something to hurt them inadvertently. I never mean to hurt anyone but that's all I seem to be doing.

Minutes drag on as I ache for Casper. Or the memories we had. I long for this cruel ache to end. It's almost like I'm stuck inside a dream, and I can't escape. I've always felt like this when I returned to Arvada. This fog or cloud hangs over me and my mind is so muddled. I want anything but this. Intuition deep down inside is telling me something I don't want to hear or admit to myself.

Everything I have ever known is ruined by a heartless king. Did this happen because I left? I never trusted Jacques and was always grateful that Vincent distanced himself a little from his father. He knows what kind of person Jacques truly is. Yet, he stands by his father as if he has no choice. Vincent always has a choice. I have to remind him of that. He can become a much better king.

He spent too much time finding me that he has to do whatever it takes to get in his father's good graces. Whatever it is, I must talk to Vincent, without upsetting him. I wonder if there's a way to convince him that things have to change. This is no way to live.

I focus on my breathing and try to ease the anger away.

Julienne assists me into a beautiful sky-blue dress. Its fitted bodice has a square neckline trimmed out in gathered lace. The sleeves are belled at the bottom and are trimmed with more lace. It's funny how much we dress up here for dinner whereas in the mortal world, the dresses are so much simpler. These are very pretty though. Julienne pulls my hair back in a curly ponytail. I wonder if the king ever did anything to her or her family.

I turn to face her. "I'm sorry if he's ever hurt you."

Her eyebrows furrow. "Ma'am?"

Someone knocks on the door and Julienne answers it.

Vincent strides in his blue army suit. Julienne curtsies and leaves. Vincent's quiet. My pulse quickens. *Stay calm.*

"You look beautiful, mon trésor."

"Thank you. You look handsome." He watches me quietly as I try to decide which necklace to wear.

Vincent comes up behind me, chooses the rope necklace and places it around my neck. His hands linger a moment and I meet his eyes in the mirror. He's bothered by something. By the twitching in his jaw, his teeth are clenched. He knows I tried to leave and that I was in the village today.

I swallow hard. "Is something wrong?"

As if he flips a switch, his lips turn up into a smile and the darkness fades from his face. "Nothing. Let's enjoy dinner."

Vincent takes my hand and leads me down to the dining hall. We sit at the main table, waiting for the King. As I look around, I notice a few military men with women I've never seen before. They appear sad, some almost to the brink of tears, some anxious and fidgeting a lot. They're in beautiful dresses, their hair is immaculately pulled back. Disgust rolls over me, knowing the King has taken villagers and gave them to his men. I clench my teeth, but I take a breath. I must remain calm and ignore it. Will I be able to talk to Vincent about it? Will he listen? Or has Jacques completely brainwashed him? These are dangerous men, and I must choose my words and actions carefully.

Once the King enters, we stand and bow or curtsey. Two women flank him, and I recognize the woman on the left. Claudette stands tall in a beautiful green flowy dress with a plunging neckline. An antique bronze necklace with a hanging cross pendant adorns her chest. Her blonde hair is slightly pulled back and several ringlets cascade over her shoulders.

My heart leaps to my throat. I want to lunge for Jacques and strangle him. How dare he take her? She has a husband and a child. Why is this happening? I want to save her but how? I can't defeat any of these people. I have to convince Vincent to end this.

When Claudette notices me, she narrows her eyes with hatred, but fear overcomes them when the King touches her back. This is my fault. I shouldn't have been speaking to them. Did anyone see us? Are there eyes all over? Does Vincent have people following me, making sure I'm doing what I'm supposed to? Perhaps he doesn't trust me and is afraid I'll run again.

"Greetings." King Jacques raises his glass. "We are celebrating the return of my son and his beloved. The Elves took her from us, but Vincent defeated them and saved them. It's only a matter of time before they are completely wiped out. Sprites will prevail."

Cheers and applause rumble inside the room. King Jacques takes Claudette, forcing a kiss on her. Gritting my teeth, I look away.

I have to do something but what? "Who is the King's mistress?" I ask Vincent after we take our seats. I keep my voice level.

"She's no one. Just some girl."

His words almost cause me to shatter in a million pieces on the table. "How can you say no one?"

His eyes hold mine. "Don't concern yourself with whatever the King does with his personal life," he whispers to me as a warning.

I'm far from finished.

After dinner, which I barely eat anything knowing how little the villagers have, we all congregate in the dance hall. Dancing is the last thing on my mind. My eyes are on Claudette. She's surrounded by guards, her lady in waiting, and of course, the King. Her eyes scan the crowd and she's very wary of anyone standing next to her. I can tell she feels out of place.

King Jacques whispers in her ear and once they make it out to the dance floor, the music begins. Everyone watches Jacques and Claudette dance for a few seconds, then they fill the floor.

Vincent stares out into the sea of dancers, stoic but I feel the tension emanating from him. He remains quiet as he watches his father and Claudette move as if they've been partners for years. I see her eyes lighten and the corners of her mouth upturn the slightest bit. Perhaps she's only being kind. Everyone here must be pleasant, or the King will behead them apparently.

The song ends and the crowd applauds. King Jacques and Claudette make their way toward us. My heart is beating fast as I remind myself to remain calm.

I curtsey as Vincent bows.

"Your Majesty," I say.

"I found a good one." King Jacques pulls Claudette close to him and she smiles. She glances at me. "This is my boy," he tells Claudette.

"Nice to meet you," she says.

Vincent's lips stretch into an easy, sexy smile. "You as well. I hope you are enjoying tonight's festivities."

"Of course."

"Vincent, might I steal Lady Megan for a dance?" King Jacques asks.

Heat rises to my cheeks. I don't want to be left alone with Jacques.

Vincent hesitates but nods. "Of course. Would you care to dance?" he asks Claudette.

"Yes."

Vincent takes her to the floor, leaving me with the King.

He raises his hands, inviting me. I clear my throat before taking his hand and placing my other on his shoulder. When his hand grasps my back right above my hip, I want to hurl.

My hands shake. A bulge forms in my throat. My heart beats a thousand miles a minute, but I try to appear calm.

"I am very happy you have returned. You make my Vincent a very happy man." His voice is low, gentle. Like a caring father.

I clear my throat. "Thank you. He makes me happy as well."

"Good."

We move along other couples on the floor. I'm amazed I haven't forgotten the steps to the dance.

"I hope you are done seeking information from the rebels."

Heat races to my cheeks.

"I am a great keeper of secrets, especially ones that benefit my boy. Whatever happened while you were away needs to be forgotten. Whatever you heard today in the village needs to be forgotten."

"Of course." Doesn't he know the Elves spelled me?

"You and Vincent are bound." Venom touches his voice. "It would be in your best interest if you adhere to the rules, for you do not want to upset your king." Disdain flickers across his face. "You are a Sprite, and you should behave as such. Vincent will one day be king, and you are to be his queen. I advise that you do him the honor of becoming his wife and that you do not hurt him again." He steps closer and whispers in my ear. "Otherwise, I will have no choice but to banish you to the village as a traitor. Or worse."

His warning sends ice throughout my body, freezing me in place and leaving me breathless. The music stops and there is applause. When he draws back, he smiles and pats my shoulder. "The fireworks will be starting soon. Don't want to miss those." King Jacques leaves the room with the crowd and I exhale, almost losing my step.

"Megan? What is it?" Vincent rushes up to me, taking my arms in his.

I shake my head. "I'm fine," but my voice is shaky and breaks. "I'm fine." I can't breathe.

"Come on." We retreat outside to the maze of bushes in front of the palace with a crowd of people preparing for the fireworks show. Everyone wants to see the pretty colors. Vincent keeps walking us away from the thick of the crowd.

"Where are we going?"

"To the hill so we can see the fireworks better."

I've upset him, and now he's going to warn me about something. I can't take him and his father. "We can see them fine from the maze."

As if he detects my hesitation, he whirls around to face me. "Megan, I don't want to argue tonight." He snaps.

Jerking me along, my pulse edges higher. What is he going to do to me? Show me who's in charge? Does he know what his father said to me?

"Vincent, what is the matter? You're hurting me."

He eases his grip. "Sorry."

I take a deep breath and turn him to face me. "What's wrong?"

A firework whirls into the sky and explodes in a kaleidoscope of vibrant colors that reflect on his face. His anger scares me.

"What were you doing in the village today, Megan? I know that's why King Jacques spoke to you."

"I was wandering around. I haven't been in a long time. I...I wanted to know what happened."

He shakes his head. "Why did you try to leave? You are not allowed down there."

I'm tired of being told what to do; where to go; how to do it. So what if I was compelled by Elves. Can't anyone trust me? The anger inside me wells. "You know what? Yeah, I tried to leave so I could find a witch to end this stupid spell because I can't stand it. Everyone thinks I'm out to betray you or the king. And you know what's even more messed up? The fact that you all are using their wives and women for whatever purpose you desire. None of the women at the table are from the palace."

Another firework thunders into the sky. Green reflects in his eyes and across his face.

He lets out a dry laugh. "They deserve what's to come to them."

I gasp. "Vincent, your father and your *friends* are raping these women. What is wrong with you? How could you stand by and let this happen?"

"You don't know what you're talking about."

"Then by all means, explain it to me. I'm so tired of you keeping everything from me like I can't handle it. Like I'm some fragile, naïve little girl. I'm not as fragile as you think."

He lets out a sigh. "I never thought you were. You have no idea what's going on. Ever since King Jacques was sworn in, they have rebelled against him. They follow their own rules or try to. They lie and manipulate to get what they want. They don't think he's fair, but he has been nothing but fair to these people. He has given them so much, yet they balk at it."

"Given them what, Vincent? Have you actually seen the way they live in the village? These women have done nothing. Neither have the men. How can you be okay with this?"

"The women are brought here to punish their husbands or whomever. The King nor the army *rapes* them, Megan. They give them a night of dancing, dinner, and pleasure. Or whatever they desire."

"You are so oblivious. You don't see how miserable these women are tonight. Every one of them were sad and scared. None of you see it. None of you care. And when you're finished with them, you dump them out forcing them to find their own way home."

His jaw twitches as he glares at me. Blue, white, red colors dance across his face. "The King would never hurt a woman or allow a woman to be hurt. You should know that."

"What is that supposed to mean? Your father—"

"The *King*," he corrects.

"The King threatened me."

"Because he's afraid you'll leave me again. What do I have to do to get you to understand?"

"Not get the King to do your bidding." I glare at him. "You're perfectly okay with him threatening me?"

"Of course not." Another firework. "He won't hurt you, but if you keep trying to play investigator, it will become harder and harder to protect you from him."

"That's all you have to say. Why do you even stay with him? You have always hated him."

"What do you want me to do, Megan?" he yells.

"Leave. Stand up for yourself. Stand up for me. Do *something*. You don't even bat an eye at what your father does or asks you to do."

"He is the King. He can do whatever he wants."

"He can be dethroned. You know he isn't good."

"I wouldn't speak ill toward the King. He saved you. He is allowing you to be at the palace with me because we are bound. If you do not follow this, there will be no protection for you, or your parents and he will do what he wants. Do you understand?"

There's weight in his words, and I realize he is protecting me. And my family. I didn't realize my family would ever be dangled in front of me. "What are you having to do for him in exchange for my safety? Doesn't he know I was compelled?"

"He doesn't believe that you were spelled."

That brings me up short. "What?"

"He believes you willingly left and that all of this is just another game."

Tears well in my eyes. No one trusts me. No one ever has. "Do you think that?"

When he doesn't answer, my chin quivers and I feel the familiar ache of my heart. "Vincent? What do you believe?"

"Yes, I believe you." But with the bright, white of a firework, I can see the doubt in his eyes.

I put my hands on both sides of his face, forcing him to look at me. "He's convinced you that I'm lying. What do I have to do to prove that I love you? Find the Jewel for you?"

He frowns. "Megan."

"I love you, Vincent. You. Not Casper. You."

He nods.

"Why are we here? I know you are miserable."

"You're wrong."

"He's always made you miserable. He's always controlled you and abused you. You are a much better person than him."

"That's not true. King Jacques is not a bad person."

"Why do you defend him? He treats you like—"

"Choose your next words carefully." Darkness clouds his eyes. "Anyone who rebels against the King will pay the consequences."

Multiple fireworks burst in the night sounding like machine guns. Once it's quiet and dark, I take Vincent's hand.

"What if he does something to me?"

"He won't."

"You don't know that. What if the army takes me?"

"That is what I am trying to prevent. I can't protect everyone. Only you and I will not let that happen to you. No one will hurt you and if they do, I will kill them. You are off limits."

His words cause me to shiver.

He escorts me back to the castle in silence and when we reach my room, he rushes me inside, closing the door.

"Megan," he says, his voice softer now. "My father has done a lot for me and I can't turn my back on him. He understands me like no one else has."

My heart drops. "Not even me?"

"It's different. He knows what I am. If that ever gets out, we are both dead. I don't like a lot of what he does but he is King, and I can't stop him. To keep you safe, he's using my secret as blackmail. I have to do what he says."

I gasp. "He would turn against his own son? Don't you see he's using you? That's all you are to him."

Hot fury flashes in his eyes. "That is out of line." He takes a deep breath and closes his eyes. Once he opens them, they are soft. "Please understand that I am protecting you. I know you spoke to the villagers, and I know they more than likely told you a lot of lies about the King. He is trying to find a Queen."

I let out a dry laugh. "By forcing married women from their husbands to be with him?"

"The King does whatever he wants."

"Then be the better King, Vincent." I make my way toward him, wrap my arms around his neck. "Do what's right. I would be proud to be your Queen. What if once we find the Jewel, we left? Just you and me. We could be happy."

Hope flashes in his eyes, then defeat. He breaks our gaze, taking my hands in his. He's conflicted. "Get some rest tonight. We will visit your parents tomorrow." He kisses my cheek and leaves, locking the door.

❧

I need to ignore the strange, heavy feeling inside me. I have to be the dutiful wife to Vincent. I must prove my love to him and convince him to become the righteous leader of the Sprites. Perhaps with me as Queen, I can save the Sprites. Vincent knows what's right. Together, we can put back together this village and palace. It will take time.

Vincent comes to my room and studies me. "Are you okay?"

"Yes, why?"

"About last night." He shakes his head as he makes his way toward me. "I shouldn't have gotten so angry. I worry over you so much. I know your brain has been messed with by an Elf and I wish I could take it away. I also don't want to have to worry about King Jacques. Do you forgive me?" He holds my hands and as I peer into his pleading blue eyes, I nod.

"Of course."

"I've been thinking about what you said last night. Of course, I want you to be my queen, but can you understand my hesitancy?"

As I search his eyes, I remember a time when we were in love. "Vincent, I'm sorry. If I could go back in time and change things, I would. I would have been more careful and never let Casper fool me." Taking a deep breath, I wrap my arms around his neck. "This is a new beginning. For us. For the Sprites."

He gazes into my eyes and leans down. My breath hitches and his lips meet mine. He's gentle as his mouth moves against mine. I keep expecting explosions, heat, or anything, but I still feel nothing. How can I make this work when I feel nothing? I'm thinking too much about it. Am I too damaged?

I pull him tighter against me, trying to mute my thoughts. Casper flashes through my mind. My heart hasn't healed, and I know this, but I have to convince Vincent.

When he draws back, he smiles. "Wow. It's as intense as I remember."

I return the smile. "I love you, Vincent. I am sorry for hurting you."

He brushes his lips across mine. "There is no need for apologies."

"Do you forgive me?"

"Always. Come on, let's go eat."

We go down for breakfast and when we reach the main hall, I come to a halt. Claudette is kissing Jacques and she's smiling. My stomach turns when I see her feed him a strawberry. What is happening? She's wearing a beautiful dress and an ornate necklace that drops to her cleavage.

"That's a first," Vincent says.

"What is?"

"No one has ever made him laugh like that."

Is Claudette playing him? I have to know. I'll find her later, but I have to be careful. I don't want it to seem like I'm fishing for information. I bide my time until I can catch her alone.

After several days, I find Claudette in a room with her lady in waiting and other court ladies. Once she sees me, she smiles. "Lady Megan, please, won't you join me?" She invites me to sit next to her and dismisses her lady in waiting.

"It is beautiful here."

"Is this real?" I ask.

Confusion crosses her eyes. "What do you mean?"

"Are you happy?"

"Of course, I am. I have all the riches; I have a man who truly understands what it means to love a woman. I am fed, clothed, bathed daily."

"What of your husband and child?"

"I do miss them, but they are being taken care of."

"How?"

"I asked the King to care for them. They won't live in the village or the palace. They are being moved to the East District. I believe close to where your parents reside."

I don't like that she knows where my parents live. "Will you see them?"

"Of course. I see Marie. King Jacques loves her. He lets her ride horses. This is good for me. I was first upset but everything I thought about King Jacques was wrong."

I nod slowly. "I am glad you are happy."

She smiles and squeezes my hand. "Everything will be fine."

"I must leave you now."

"Of course. Give my best to Prince Vincent."

"I will."

As I make my way to my room, I'm baffled. Is this all a ploy? Is she happy? Is this another manipulation trick by King Jacques? He is so good at it. I have to get out of this brainwashed insanity. What did she mean that everything would be fine? Is she plotting against the king? Is she going to kill him?

Ten

hunder rolls in the distance as Vincent and I ride in the carriage after the royal wedding. It lived up to its hype. King Jacques and Queen Claudette were married in a grand celebration. Now I must wait until the king dies. If I'm right about Claudette. It's been weeks and I've fallen back into a routine. I have done all that I can to prove to Vincent that my love for him is real. I have been his abiding bride. Holding my head high as if I were never kidnapped at all. The gossip has stopped. While I have returned to my being a Sprite, I try so hard to ignore the uneasy, foggy feeling. I still feel nothing when Vincent kisses me, and I hate it.

We still haven't found the Jewel and I wonder what it's doing to Vincent and how much time he has left. He doesn't talk about it, and he doesn't even want to find the witch to end the spell. I don't understand.

I glance at Vincent, asleep in the carriage. So peaceful. I love him and I want to make him happy. I don't understand why he doesn't want that.

Thunder rumbles again.

Vincent shifts and something glints against his neck. Carefully, I lean over and my entire body freezes.

Black, speckled jewel. Variegated in color.

The Nuummite Jewel.

Vincent is wearing it.

My breath catches in my throat as I sit back in my seat. My heart hammers wildly against my chest. A sudden chill hits me. The trees pass by in a blur of lies and deceit.

He lied. He's had it this whole time. Why would he not tell me? No wonder he never wanted to search for it. He never gave it up.

Was the vision I saw even real? What happened in the rest of it? Did he kill Casper and take it back? Why would he lie to me about having it? Even if he killed Casper, why wouldn't he want to gloat about it? I would have.

What am I not seeing? What am I missing?

Staring at the Jewel, I think about my life here. How much I've been pretending. How much I try ignoring that heavy unease.

I want to leave. I want to return to the mortal world. I've never had this strong of a feeling, but I don't belong here and the more I give in to these feelings, the more it feels right. Is that why I've been feeling like this?

I rub my eyes. I need to see the vision again. Or something.

Carefully reaching for Vincent's hand, praying that I don't wake him, I touch him.

"I will find her," Casper says, on the beach.

"Not if you're dead."

"She's a possession to you. Like the Jewel. You've never loved her and the moment you think you have her, you won't want her."

"You don't know anything."

"I know I love her, and she'll know that you shot her."

"No! I was aiming for you!"

Casper shakes his head. "She'll know you manipulated her into loving you because you think she's weak and you think no one will ever love you."

I jerk my hand away from Vincent. He shot me.

I am a naïve, gullible girl. I've been stupid. I don't know what or who to believe anymore. They both want me dead.

I have to get out of here. I can find the witch and she can end the compulsion. I'll give her the Jewel. Then I can go back home.

Why would Vincent hide this? Why hasn't he told me or shown me what happened after the exchange? What's he hiding from me?

I try to even my breath. I have to think about this. I have to steal the Jewel. Once I steal it, I can figure out the rest later.

Vincent can't know I know he has it. I have to catch him off guard.

A clap of thunder echoes across the horizon and I flinch.

Vincent wakes.

Once I peer into the sky, a dark wall of clouds slowly travels over us. The wind picks up, carrying dust and other particles in the air.

"We need to find shelter," Vincent says.

I turn to him. "We can't make it to the palace?"

Lightning flashes in the distance and thunder erupts.

"Sir, the storm is coming," Godfrey, the driver, shouts.

"We have to make it back to the castle or at least to my parents." I can't catch my breath. The heavy sound of my heartbeat thrashes in my ear. Dizziness overcomes me and my body trembles.

Vincent squeezes my hand. "Megan, it's okay. We don't have time to make it to either place."

"The storm is coming, and you don't want to be caught in it." The look he gives me tells me it's going to be a mesocyclone. They happen once or twice a year here. Storms so powerful they become destructive. We have no shelter and I know he's right. We have to hurry and find one before we die. I've always hated storms, but lately any loud noise makes me jump and panic.

Lightning cracks nearby, exploding in a flash of bright light. The ground shakes as the carriage careens sideways throwing me against the roof. I hear the horse neigh and speed down the road. The horse drags us and there's nothing I can grip to prevent myself from being flung all around.

We crash into something. The carriage breaks open. My ears ring and I can feel blood trickle down my face. Everything spins around me, and I feel sick.

The heavy rain starts, sounding like the roar of an ocean wave.

"Megan, are you okay?" Vincent shouts.

"I think so."

He kicks open the door making it large enough for us to fit. Slipping through, he turns around and lifts me out of the carriage. Holding my head, I watch the horse gallop away into the night. Godfrey is nowhere to be found.

Wind knocks into me, and I stumble. It sends my hair lashing across my face. I'm so dizzy I need to lie down. I'm soaking wet and there is no shelter.

"Come on, Megan. We have to get out of here."

Squinting through the dust and wind and rain, we're in an open field with trees scarcely around. Black and furious clouds churn above us illuminated by lightning.

"Where are we going?"

"We'll find a place."

He takes my hand, and we hurry to find a safe place.

My life is nothing but running. Always away from something or someone trying to kill me. Is this it? Am I going to die in a storm? I can't run in this storm, but I need the Jewel. It's now or never. It's Vincent and me. Alone.

I don't care. Storm or no storm, tonight, that Jewel will be mine.

Eleven

When I smell the sweet scent of a Lily of the Valley flowers, I spot them up ahead. It's a beautiful flower with bell shaped flowers and orange-red berries that are extremely toxic. I've always loved the scent and Vincent would always bring them to me.

Vincent is running faster than me, and I release my hand from his. "Megan!"

"It's okay. I'm right behind you. Find us a place."

He nods.

Running in this ridiculous dress proves to be difficult but I manage. It's heavy and the rain makes it worse. I swear one day, I'm going to pack extra clothes for running.

The wind picks up more and Vincent leads the way to wherever we're going. He looks back occasionally. I fall behind slightly and tear off what I can of the Lily of the Valley, making sure some berries come with them and shove them in my dress.

Rain continues to gush out of the sky and wind carries it sideways. Lightning strikes, and Vincent seizes my hand, pulling me closer to him. The storm is unyielding.

"There!" Vincent yells, pointing in the thick rain. "We can stay there for the night."

I can barely make out an abandoned stone cottage as we run towards it. I hope it provides some protection. We reach the cottage, soaking wet and panting.

"Let me see if I can start a fire," Vincent says.

It's incredibly dark in here and the sinister sounds of the storm only add to the fear reverberating throughout me. I rummage through some drawers in the kitchen and find candles by some incredible luck. We gather sheets and whatever we can find to cover the pane-less windows from the raging storm. We both know it won't protect much but it's something.

I never worried too much about these storms, since I had always been in the safety of the castle but being in this dilapidated cottage makes me uneasy. At least it's stone but it still doesn't provide a lot of protection. The storm shouldn't get bad until later.

"I know it's a long shot but see if you can find any food," he says.

I guess it's his way of keeping our minds off the storm and I'm glad he let me choose the food. I hope I can find something to put the berries from the Lily of the Valley in for Vincent to consume. I don't want to kill him, but I may not have a choice, given that I need the Jewel. Plus, he shot me.

The kitchen is adjacent to the main room, and it looks like whoever lived here before rushed out. Or soldiers took advantage. The chairs around the table were all on their sides, trash littered the floor, and an unsurmountable volume of dust topped the countertops.

I rummage through the cabinets for food but there isn't much. A few unopened cans but when I find half of a bottle of absinthe, I gasp, hoping Vincent doesn't hear me.

Grabbing a couple of glasses, I wipe them the best I can and crush the berries in my hand, letting their juices drip in one of the glasses. I pour some absinthe in both. I try to wipe the berry residue from my hand, but the red color stained it.

"Find anything?"

He startles me but I recover quickly. "I found this," I say holding it out to him.

He cocks an eyebrow. "Absinthe?"

I shrug and take a drink. "Why not?" I swallow and almost cry out from the burn.

Vincent chuckles. "Take it easy. Are you sure you want to be drinking this? It can cause some craziness."

No more than what you make me feel. "Come on. Don't be scared. Why don't we get wasted tonight? Since we're stuck here anyway." I drink a little more, feeling the burn in my stomach and my veins. I don't want any more, but I have to keep up the charade. I hope this doesn't backfire.

Staring at me as if he's accepting my challenge, he reaches for the other glass. He raises it in a toast and swallows all of the absinthe with the berries.

I refill his glass with a little more and smile.

"Trying to get me drunk?"

"Maybe. Come on. What's it gonna hurt? Besides, we never do anything this fun. We're always so serious."

He drinks it.

The warmth of the alcohol courses through my veins and I'm feeling good. "It feels so good getting out of that palace. Too bad we don't have a radio. Ugh. I miss music."

He laughs. "You're wasted already."

I shrug and take his hand as I start dancing around. The dress weighs me down, so I strip right out of it and I'm in my undergarments, which still covers me up. I have to keep moving so I don't fall asleep.

Vincent stumbles and falls to the ground near the fireplace, taking me with him. We laugh, not caring that there's a storm raging outside.

Deep down inside, I want him to fall into it. I want the fire to destroy him the way he destroyed me. I hate these thoughts in my head. This isn't who I am. I want out of this misery.

He sits up and shakes his head. "That stuff is strong."

I sit next to him, against a faded and musty couch. And I wait. I wait for him to fall asleep.

Something's on his mind but he remains silent. Unless it's the berries and absinthe messing with his mind already. It's not like him to be so quiet, there's no telling what goes on inside Vincent's mind.

"I can't believe the King is married," he says.

"He seems happy."

"Yeah."

"Does it ever bother you to keep so many secrets from me?" I blurt. I'm so drunk and I don't care what I'm saying.

"What?"

I shake my head. "I guess I'll always be a fragile, insignificant girl to you. You think I'm out to get you and you always say that everything you do is for me and with me in mind. But it's not."

"Jesus, what are you talking about? I'm too drunk for this conversation."

"Why lie about the Jewel, Vincent? I was willing to go fight the Elves for you—but you already had it. Is this how it's going to be? Am I supposed to go along and not have a mind of my own? Let you do whatever you want like your father. Be the quiet girl in the corner. Your abiding bride who says nothing and does nothing."

He shakes his head. "Stop overreacting. My men found the Jewel the other day and brought it to me. I didn't have time to talk about it because we were busy with the wedding. Plus, I didn't wanna argue with you."

Whatever. I'm sick of the lies. I'm sick of feeling this way.

The rest of the evening, we warm ourselves in front of the fire, listening to the growling storm. The winds are strong enough to rip the cabin to pieces and take us with it. I hope it will soon die down so I can leave. My plan must work. As soon as Vincent passes out, I will snatch the Jewel and flee.

At some point, when the embers burn low, I look at Vincent and realize he's asleep. His head leans against the crumbling couch and he breathes steadily. I thought for sure the berries would make him sick, but the absinthe was strong enough to put him to sleep before the berries could activate.

The rain picks up again, masking the heavy thumping of my heartbeat. I inch away from him, silently. Holding my breath, I spot the beautiful Jewel across his chest hanging on a thin black rope. This small Jewel has cost so much heartache and lives.

I need to grab it as fast as I can and run.

Reaching for it, I swallow hard, though my throat is parched. The alcohol is messing with me, and my hands shake.

I take a deep breath and exhale slowly and quietly.

I rip the necklace from his neck and stand on wobbly knees. Dizziness blurs my vision for a moment.

Bolting from the cabin, the cold rain pelts me as I flee into the woods. I don't know where I'm going. I just run. It's so cold but I don't let that stop me. I have to get the Jewel to its rightful place.

As I run into the harsh winds and rain, my heart pounds. I feel so alive but I'm not free yet. I know he'll wake soon and come find me. The wind makes it difficult to run in a straight line, but I keep going. I keep pushing my legs, gripping the Jewel and my freedom as tightly as I can.

"Megan!" I hear Vincent scream, but it's muffled. "Come on! This isn't funny."

My heart knocks into my ribs as I pick up the pace. How is he awake? Is he immune? Will he pass out soon? Can he not be killed?

Lightning strikes nearby causing me to jump.

"Megan! Come back!"

I find a tree with a hollow opening and hide inside. Lightning flashes every ten seconds followed by deafening thunder. It blazes once more and I'm flying high in a cloudless, sunny sky. My wings flap as I watch the world below me race by. With the wind in my face and the sun warming my skin, I'm free as I glide with no worries.

"Megan! You can't hide from me."

I blink several times and look around. I'm back inside the tree with the storm around me and Vincent screaming my name. I don't know what happened, but I need to get away. Vincent comes closer and I hold my breath, hoping he can't sense the Jewel somehow. I hold it tightly in my hands as I watch his dark shadow move through the thick rain, frantically searching for me. I hide as deep into the tree as I can, hoping the lightning won't give me away.

The rain falls sideways in sheets. Every few seconds, wind gusts through the rain creating chaos in its wake and I hope it doesn't take my tree with it. Thunder echoes like constant chimes on a clock. Like I'm Cinderella and I have to get to my destination before the clock strikes twelve.

Once Vincent disappears deeper into the woods, I wait for a few minutes, wondering what I imagined. I was flying. The skin looked more like scales as if it was a dragon. Why did I imagine myself as a dragon? It was so real.

I gasp and shake my head. I can't think of that right now. I wait before I make my move. I have to be completely sure Vincent won't find me.

Slowly peeking out from the tree, I try to see any movement and when I'm absolutely sure, I take off to the left. Away from Vincent. Away from the hell. Toward freedom.

Twelve

The next morning, I wake with a start. My head aches and I'm congested. My eyes weigh a thousand pounds and my muscles ache like I got hit by a Mack truck. Sometime in the night, I found an underground shelter but the storm and fear of being found kept me awake.

Needless to say, I didn't sleep at all.

I have once again escaped. I must find my way to the witch. Part of me wants to see if I can return the Jewel to the Elves. Hoping to see Casper so we can unite. I get to my feet, staring down at my tattered and damp undergarments. The shoes are uncomfortable but at least I'm wearing some. I remember the last time I wore the dress, the one that

I shucked out of last night, I met Casper for the first time.

I had been strolling in the vast rose garden inside the palace with Florence. There was a light breeze in the air, and we had paper fans to cool us. Our arms were linked as we walked, and once I saw him, I halted, my breath catching in my throat. I covered my face, except my eyes, with my fan.

When the man locked eyes with me, my heart palpitated. I turned to Florence. "Who is that?"

She looked up and saw the man. "I don't know but he and his friend are handsome."

Heat pricked beneath my cheeks as I realized I had not noticed the other man. The blond-haired man seemed to have taken away my breath. My eyes flicked back to his and I felt a strange pull toward him. I wasn't sure if it was the intense way he looked at me.

"Perhaps they'll be at tonight's party." Florence's voice broke the intense staring contest. She guided me toward the palace and when I turned back, his gaze was still on me.

Later that evening, I fretted over what to wear to the party, not even knowing for sure if he would be there. I decided to wear a velvet maroon dress and my hair partially pulled back with curls. I couldn't understand my nervousness. Was it because I was so lonely and missed Vincent that I yearned for attention or was it something else?

I made my way to the party and found Florence. We danced a few songs with some of our usual friends, but I didn't see the man. I shouldn't have been looking for him anyway.

Disappointed, I walked outside to take a break from the dancing. The night was warm and the air thick, almost suffocating. I took a seat on a bench, fanning myself. I was feeling oddly sad that I hadn't seen the man tonight. I couldn't understand the feelings that stirred inside me when I saw him. It was wrong of me to feel such a way. I sighed and got up from the bench. I walked back into the palace and as I was about to enter the great hall, I looked back but bumped into someone.

As I turned my head to apologize, I met his eyes. His hands were on my arms, frozen in place. Desire and a mesmerizing look held in the most beautiful brown eyes I had ever seen. They looked so innocent. My body trembled and my heart was frenzied. I couldn't tear my eyes away and I don't know how long we stood like that.

He released me, embarrassed and with a tender smile he said, "Hi. My name is Casper." His voice was smooth like satin and all I wanted was to hear more. "May I have your name?"

"Megan," I told him without hesitation.

"Would you care for a dance?"

"Yes."

When he touched me, I didn't want him to let go. I felt safe. Comfortable. Like I was where I was supposed to be. He told me later that he was an Elf. I thought at the time that he was proving his trust in me, that he loved me.

The cool, drafty morning breeze brings me back to the dreaded present. The storm passed eventually, leaving the sky brighter, the air crisper and the sun shinier. Even though my body aches and I'm exhausted, I take a deep breath and I feel lighter. A little freer. I can breathe again. My body isn't shaking from anxiety as much. I feel relaxed and less on edge. I'm still not in the clear but I'm away from Vincent and that's a victory in and of itself.

As I travel, I place the Jewel around my neck and it glows for a second, causing me dizziness for a moment. The Nuummite Jewel is not meant for Sprites, and I can only imagine what it does to Sprites who wear it. Except Vincent but he's half Elf. Maybe it's still the effects of the absinthe I drank last night. That's why I imagined myself as a dragon. Absinthe is crazy and I never want to experience that again.

I slow my pace as a sluggish fog begins to settle in the forest but as I pass several black trees with no leaves, I realize it's smoke. The ground is soft, wet, and black. The smoke burns my lungs dries out my eyes. My heart races as the further I walk, the thinner the forest becomes until I reach a clearing. This didn't used to be a clearing. The beautiful lush green forest that I had grown to love was once full of animals running around like some fairytale I read as a child. The trees expanded heights and widths no person could ever fathom. The forest thrived under the sun yet buried secrets throughout. Secrets only the animals knew.

But now, the forest is gone. Half burned trees still bleed smoke. Something other than smoke fills the air and I gasp. In between downed trees, charred bodies scatter. There is so much death. I hold my breath from the putrid stench of seared flesh. Charcoal mixed with a sulfurous odor lingers in the air. It makes me sick. There are no animals. There isn't a single sound, except the quiet burning of the stumps. This war has continued because of this Jewel. If the Elves have it, what's to say the Sprites won't steal it again?

I carefully make my way across the deserted battlefield, hoping a gunman or a land mine won't kill me. I hate that I have to avoid stepping on dead men. My stomach churns from the sight and smells. I push forward through the eerie silence and after a few hours of walking, I find a small cottage with a thatched roof. It looks well-kept and I wonder if anyone lives here. I want to evade all people until I reach the witch but I'm tired and I need food. The thought of returning to the human world excites me.

I knock on the door, but no one answers. Peering inside through the windows, it doesn't look abandoned. They're gone. Off to war. Or gathering food. There isn't a neighbor for miles. The cottage is surrounded by lush, overgrown gardens and beautiful trees that hover above.

Taking a deep breath, I creep inside the cottage. If someone returns, I can explain who I am, though I don't want word to get back to Vincent on my whereabouts. It's a quaint cottage with wooden furniture. A fireplace with a pile of wood nearby. Dust is caked on every piece of furniture and tabletop. The smell of must and mold is strong the deeper I move inside. The sunlight barely filters through the dusty windows. It's clear no one has lived here in a while, or they refused to clean. As I wander into the bedroom, I gasp. I see a man lying on the bed with a gun in his hand and blood splattered across the wall behind the bed. I close my eyes and push the nausea away. War is never a pretty thing. Sadly, it looks fairly recent.

Once I steady myself, I walk across the room to the closet and find a sheet. I cover the man, though I contemplate taking his gun. I don't know how to use one. Inside the chest, there are clothes, though all men's clothes. No jeans. I don't know why I thought there would be. I miss wearing jeans. I pull a pair of pants and a shirt from the drawers and immediately change. The clothes hang a little loose on me, but they'll work. I close the door to the man's room and try not to think about a dead body being here. I'll burn my clothes.

I need shelter and I need to rest, though I'm not sure I'll be able to. I know Vincent is looking for me and if he hasn't already, he'll gather a group to search for me. I need to find a bag or something and bring supplies with me.

When I meander into the kitchen, I search the cabinets for anything. I don't care what it is. It's a shame canned food hasn't been invented yet. I remember in my human life getting off work trying to find something to eat and balking at the canned soup. Now, I long for that. Or even Jonathan bringing me a bag of fast food.

I almost cry out when I see fruit and vegetables in the cabinets. I don't know how much longer I can stay but I have to get to the Elves and somehow figure out how to find them. I eat an apple and put aside some vegetables for me to make a soup.

Light flashes and I stumble, as if the ground were shaking. I walk into a room and meet a man who looks familiar. Jacques, I realize.

"Vincent," he says, looking at me.

Am I Vincent? Is this a memory? Did Vincent find me and is putting images in my head?

"She's gone," I say, but it's Vincent's voice. "She left with that Elf. She doesn't want me, Father!"

His father's stoic stance softens for a second, but he recovers. "What of the Jewel?"

Vincent clenches his fists and I feel his anger as if it's my own. "It's fine. Why do you care so much?"

"You know why, Vincent. You must keep it to protect you. You must learn to contain the dragon. For now, at least."

"What's the point? I am ready. Megan left me. What do I have left?"

"You don't need her. She deserted you. Find a new girl."

"I don't want anyone else. I love her. Don't you understand that part of me is Elf?"

"Unfortunately, I do."

That hurts. "She left because she's been spelled."

"If that's what you need to tell yourself to sleep at night."

I hate him. Why can't he see how much pain I'm in? Why doesn't he care?

He shakes his head. "If you love this girl so damn much, then why haven't you married her? Use the Jewel to your advantage. Do whatever you must to bring her back. Kill the Elf if you have to. She's yours, not his. Be a man. But if you bring her back, you'd better erase her memories."

Blinking several times, I'm back in the cottage, lying on the floor. I don't understand what that was.

Did I have a vision of Vincent and Jacques? How could I? Has Vincent found me?

I get to my feet searching outside through each window in each room. I see nothing, nor do I hear anything. Why did I have a vision? It wasn't even mine. How could I have seen that?

The Jewel is warm against my skin. I remove it, and as I stare at the beautiful, mesmerizing Jewel, it glints in the light and feels warm in my hands. Its variegated color is quite unique as it shows black with specks of gold and blue.

How much truth has been hidden from me? What is the truth behind this unique Jewel? Did the Jewel give me a vision? Vincent's always been the one to show visions, now I wonder if it's because of the Jewel. Do I have a power now? Something about the vision comes back to me. Vincent has to keep the Jewel to stop the dragon. What does that mean? Can it show me the vision of when Vincent and Casper did the exchange?

Casper. My heart aches for him. I know I shouldn't, but I can't help it. I can't stop thinking about him. I know it wasn't real for him, but it was for me. Every moment. Every kiss. Every touch. Every life. All of it was real for me.

Thirteen

lutching the Nuummite, I close my eyes willing it to show me the exchange, but nothing happens. I try a few more times, still, nothing. Is Vincent able to send me messages with it?

I shake my head. I will make soup and stay the night.

Putting the Jewel in my pocket, I start cutting up the vegetables. I always hated cooking, now I find it quite relaxing. Ron never helped with that. Always saying something about how bad it was. I miss my human mom, and also maman. I wish I could see her, but Vincent would find me. I hate that I left her again, but she has to know I can't survive here.

I yearn to pull out my phone and start texting Cherry. I miss her. Of all my human lives, she's been the best friend I ever had. I wonder if I'll ever see her again.

Once I chop all the vegetables, I put it all together in the cast iron pot over the fireplace. I'm not sure how long it'll take. I miss having a microwave and an oven. Or electricity.

I sigh as I sit in the chair watching the flames heat the soup pot. Watching them lick the sides, like in Vincent's basement. He shot me so he could bring me back.

Casper. Every time I see the hollow look in his eyes when he handed me over, an ache twists inside my chest. I take a deep breath before the tears consume me. I close my eyes and I'm pulled into another vision where Jacques stares at me.

"You're sure he's dead?" he asks.

Annoyed, I pinch the bridge of my nose. "Yes, Father, I shot him. He is dead."

"And Lady Megan?"

"When she wakes, she'll have no memory of him."

"Good."

I'm glad that I pleased my father. I hate removing Megan's memories. Even if they are of a disgusting Elf. I only want her to love me. She's all I have but she doesn't want me and I'm not sure she ever did. She doesn't realize that I, too, am an Elf and she is the only one I love. Perhaps, she will come back to me once she wakes. The fact that Megan ran off with one of them sickens me to my core. My heart ached for her. How could she do that to me? I did everything for her. I gave her everything. What has he ever done for her? Kidnap her and force her to a life on the run? He had to have brainwashed her. I can't let her out of my sight any longer. I need to have eyes on her constantly. Now that the Elf is dead, she is safely at home with me.

"You should propose to her soon," Father says. "Get this marriage on the way. You've waited too long for it."

"I'm trying."

"You have had several years, son."

"We've been at war all those years, Father. I've been gone so long she doesn't even know who I am anymore. I forced her into that Elf's arms with my absences."

My father's hand connects with my face. "Enough of that nonsense. Marry her or I will force you."

"You don't have to force me."

"Good. Once you marry her, I can become king and we can release the dragons and let them end the Elves."

I hate that he only sees me as a weapon against the Elves. I want them dead just as much, but I am more than just a weapon.

When the vision ends, I sit up straighter in my chair, unsure of what to think. Jacques is behind all of it. How much of Vincent's actions are because of his father or himself? His ego has definitely taken over.

There's a pounding in my head and my body is weary. Exhaustion is beginning to take over. Are the visions making me worse? I sink to the floor as the room spins around me. I try blinking the dizziness away but everything doubles.

My heart beats fast as I lie down. Pain grips my stomach. I have no idea what's happening to me unless I accidentally drank the absinthe with the poisonous berries and that's why I'm seeing visions. Vincent is always two steps ahead of me. Does he know I poisoned him? Is he immune since he's a mixed breed? Did he drug me again?

What the hell is wrong with me? Nausea rolls in my stomach as heat pours over me. Grasping my stomach, wishing for the tightness to end, it doesn't.

Lying down, I squeeze my eyes shut, focusing on my breathing until I fall asleep.

When I wake, I'm groggy like I took Benadryl or something. I want to sleep more. My soup still cooks in the fireplace. I must be more exhausted that I thought. It's the only reason for the visions. Isn't it?

I pull out the Jewel from my pocket. It warms in my hand and a strange feeling overcomes me. I feel weightless. *My wings flap and I feel free. I've been held hostage for so long. I can only fly at night when no one can see me. I ache to fly over the Belle Palais and spread fire, burning every single one of them. It would be so easy.*

But I can't.

Not yet.

I know Megan wishes I could be with her more. I need to let the dragon free before it becomes a problem. Flying over the world high above the clouds relaxes me. I can be myself up here. No one is trying to kill me. No one can hurt me.

The flight doesn't last as long as I need it to. I return to the castle, eager to see Megan, but I long to be the dragon.

"Vincent!" she yells, running toward me. "Vincent, I saw something."

I freeze. "What is it?"

"I saw a dragon. I know I saw one. Flying over us."

"Dragon? Megan, they don't exist."

She shakes her head and I know I'm going to have to remove this memory from her mind. She's insistent about these things. "I know what I saw."

"Okay. Have you told anyone else?"

"No, I'm telling you now. We need to do something. Are we in danger?"

I pull her into an embrace, holding her tight, and hating myself for what I'm about to do. "Megan, everything is okay." I place my hand on her head and will the memories to escape her mind. It's for the best. If she ever knew dragons existed, I'm not sure how to explain anything to her. I already lost her, and I will not lose her again. She is mine, only mine. If this is the way to keep her, so be it.

When I come to, there are tears in my eyes. Vincent is the dragon. I remember seeing a dragon in the sky that night. I had returned home and as I looked up in the sky, I saw the black giant soaring above. He removed my memory of it.

But now I remember.

I sit up, feeling less dizzy but still sick. I'm too lethargic to leave. Staring at the Jewel, I realize it's connected to Vincent. It was created for me, he said. It's making me see things. Like Vincent is able to do with me. I swallow hard. Is he linked to me? Can he still provide visions even though we aren't near each other?

Or is it the Jewel? I can't hold the Jewel any longer. I set it down on the table next to me, trying to ignore it.

These visions are messing with my head, and I don't understand them.

Taking a deep breath, I find a bowl from the kitchen and scoop some soup into it. I have to eat and regain some strength. If the Jewel does cause these visions, how am I going to bring it to the witch? I can't keep passing out along the way.

As I eat the soup, I can't stop staring at the Jewel. What other secrets does it hold? What else will it tell me? I can't ignore it and my curiosity overpowers me. Grabbing the Jewel, I let it warm my hands. Slowly, I get to my feet and become wobbly again. Steadying myself against the wall, I fall into another vision, or a memory of Vincent's.

The vortex ends, tossing me to the ground hard. I hear the distant sound of guns firing and men shouting. The century's old war is still happening in Arvada. The vortex made me slightly lightheaded, and I see Megan's unconscious body near a cliff. Her wound is beginning to heal.

I hear a moan and when I get to my feet, I see Casper rolling onto his back. I swear, no matter how many times I try to kill him, he survives. He thinks I'm going to exchange the Jewel for Megan but right before the vortex, I shot him.

"What did you do?" he screams as he holds his wound.

"What had to be done."

He glances behind me and rushes toward Megan. *"Megan, wake up."*

"Give it up already. I know you don't love her. It's all a ruse."

"I have always loved her! I always will."

"I guess that makes two of us. We all know I'm the better man."

"You shot her. You sent Adam to attack her, not me."

He's right but I did what I had to do. I'll fix that vision for her in case she ever sees it. Excitement thrums through my veins as I watch the blood ooze out of his skin. Disgust rolls over me watching him touch her. Hate emanates inside me. This Elf manipulated her. Stole her away from me. Turned her against me. And I'll be damned if he ever touches her again.

Clenching my teeth, I tackle Casper knocking him on his back. My fist connects with his jaw, and he punches me in the side, disabling me for a moment. When I get to my feet, I pull out my gun, but Casper is right there struggling with me.

I squeeze the trigger and Casper falls over. It's only a flesh wound, but it's enough to knock him out. Grabbing his legs, I drag his body toward the cliff. I will kill him once and for all. Megan will be mine and we can finally live happily together.

The Elf must die. Let the other Elves know I killed him. I'm out of breath. I must hurry before Megan wakes. I don't have the power anymore to erase her mind because she's too strong now. Lifting Casper's *heavy body above my head, without hesitation, I throw him over the ledge, watching with pleasure as his body slams into the water.*

Screaming as I come out of the vision, my knees give out on me and my heart drops to my stomach. I throw the Jewel across the room. A wave of pain washes over me. It feels like a hole has been pummeled into my chest. I can't catch my breath. I can't stop shaking. The tightness in my stomach returns as I choke on my tears.

Vincent killed Casper. For good. Numbness overtakes me. This isn't happening. The witch. She has to know a way to bring Casper back. This can't be over. He can't be dead. He can't. He still cared for me. Vincent somehow messed with his own visions to show me a fake one. How is that possible?

I pound my fist against the floor.

No matter how hard I hit the floor or how loud I scream, the pain is still there. I can't stop shaking. The weakness settles in once again.

It's cold, dark, and lonely in this cottage. He's truly gone. Casper *died*. A piece of me is dead. The tears are endless, and I don't know what to do.

I curl up against the hard-wooden floor, aching for solace but I find none.

Fourteen

The Jewel is buried in the ashes from the fireplace. I can't stand to see anymore visions. I've tried to rest the past few days at the cottage but the vast emptiness I feel is tearing me up. I keep thinking about the memories of Casper and me. Every kiss. Every embrace. Every smile. Everything. My eyes are raw. My throat burns. My heart is broken.

I must return the Jewel to the Elves. They can help me defeat King Jacques. They can destroy the Jewel. Then, I can leave this place forever. Now that my strength is back, I have to leave.

My shoulders slump as I stare at the fireplace. I don't even want to touch the damn Jewel. I don't want it near me. I reluctantly sift through the ashes. When

I see it, fear hits the bottom of my stomach, knowing that it will force more visions and thoughts. I need to push through and fight. I must do this. Whatever I have to do, I will do it in order to end this. I'm not sure how this journey is going to work. Perhaps I can leave the Jewel here, find the Elves and return.

I know that won't work. They'll think I'm tricking them.

I take a deep breath and grab the Jewel with a shaky hand. It warms my hand and I try to fight any thought or vision. I have to be strong. I can't let him take over my mind anymore.

No one has come back to the cottage, and I need to get moving. I pack a bag of essentials and after talking myself into it, I take the man's gun. I leave the comfort of the cottage and head east toward Belle Palais, the Elf homeland.

The day is crisp and bright, but the forest is still empty and eerie. Remains of the fire decrease, the further I walk. The shoes are big on my feet, but I don't care. It's better than being barefoot. The woods are too quiet and each time I step on a large twig, I jerk and scan the area. Paranoia sets in.

The familiar unsettling feeling that a vision is about to take over hits me. I try to fight it but it's useless. I quickly rush toward some bushes and wait.

"Where is she?" Jacques asks.

"I don't know." I know it isn't the answer my father wants but it's all I can give. I can't believe Megan tried to poison me. Why does she think I'm the enemy? I'm trying to save her.

I'm sweating and shaking. I can't catch my breath. I'm withdrawing from the Jewel and Megan is seeing everything. All the truth. She will definitely not want me after she learns that I killed Casper for good. She shouldn't have fallen for him. She should've known what would happen.

She can't be with the Elves. They destroyed me, forcing me to be a dragon. They need to die.

"How could you let her steal the Jewel? In all these years?"

"She poisoned me. I wasn't expecting her to do that."

"She's in love with an Elf. She'll do anything to get away from you and now she knows the truth."

"I can erase her mind."

"No, you can't," he yells. "Her mind has grown strong from knowing too much."

"I can do it! I will."

"You have to kill her, Vincent."

It's like he stabbed me straight through the heart with those words. "What?"

"She knows too much and won't change. You know she will try to convince those Elves."

"They'll never believe her."

"You have to kill her."

"No. Never."

He grabs me by the shirt, glaring into my eyes. "If your mother can abandon you and me, then you can let Megan go. It's a myth that Elves only love one person. You should know what a ridiculous notion that is."

"It's true."

He shakes me. "Find her and that Jewel. We will execute her. You can find another who will mind you as she should."

"Father—"

"Vincent, I will hear no more of this. She will die. That is final."

I can't kill Megan. The thought sickens me. She's compelled. She loves me. She has to.

My eyes pop open and I look around, realizing I'm lying in the middle of the forest. I sit up, my heart pounding. They're going to kill me. I have to get out of here. Scrambling to my feet, I start to run but the further I get, the more I don't want to go. There is a strong force like chains wrapped around me pulling me back, preventing me from moving further. My legs feel as if I'm trying to walk through water. The weakness returns.

I start to feel it in my heart, too. I don't want to go. It isn't right. It belongs to the Sprites, to Vincent so he won't become the dragon. He needs it to live, and I must save him.

I halt. What am I thinking? Why am I having these thoughts? What is going on? Is Vincent trying to control me? How is he doing this? I have to ignore it.

I take another step toward Belle Palais but stop again. I can't fight this feeling. I can't ignore it. It's too strong and I'm unable to move forward. The Jewel is ours. It belongs to Vincent.

Turning around, I head west. My heart pounds faster as I walk, feeling the relief as I walk in this direction. I need to move faster. I feel the urgency to get the Jewel to Vincent as quickly as I can. He's becoming weaker by the moment. The Jewel gives him strength and he's almost dead, and I must save him. I can't let him die. The Jewel directs me in the path I need to follow. It's linked to Vincent. It's a part of him.

My heart hurts at the thought of Vincent dying. I love him. He can't die. Not him.

Clenching my teeth as I try with no hope to fight the thoughts, I pick up my pace. I shake my head. I try to throw the Jewel, but it doesn't work. I'm like a magnet to it.

As I reach a point in the middle of the woods, several men stand around as if they are waiting for me. The pulling feeling has stopped, and King Jacques emerges from behind the men.

Air traps in my lungs.

"Lady Megan. How wonderful it is to see you again." He carries himself like a man who is never in a hurry.

I want to speak but I can't.

"I see you have the Jewel. Would you kindly return it?"

Behind the men, I see Vincent lying on the ground, pale and sickly. I'm sure I look just as bad. He looks as if he's about to die. If this is what it takes, then I will refuse the Jewel.

I shake my head.

"I'm not sure you heard me correctly. Would you kindly return the Jewel?" he asks once more.

I shake my head again, but my arm rises involuntarily and the Jewel dangles from my fingers. Staring at King Jacques, he winks at me. He controlled my arm. I can't believe Jacques has the power to make me do this. If he can force my body to do whatever he wants, what else can he force me to do?

He gently takes the Jewel from my hand, and I feel the heavy weight lift from me. I don't feel so dark or gloomy, and I can already feel myself getting stronger.

"Thank you. Vincent will be glad you have returned. My boy is sick, as you can see because of you. Though, looks like you know what he's going through seeing as how you look like him. Unfortunately, I don't think you can be saved this time."

My heart jumps to my throat. "What?"

Fear engulfs me, and I don't like the stern looks from the men.

"Take her."

Two men grab me, removing my bag and gun. No matter how hard I fight them, they overpower me. Placing a dark cloth over my head, I scream, and they tie my hands together. I can't fight them. The Jewel made me too weak. There is no escaping this.

Fifteen

A cockroach crawls across the cold, stone floor. Its antennas twitch once it stops. I don't even flinch. Thinking about Savannah sniffing a roach once, then running away makes me chuckle. I miss that little dog. A tear slides down my cheek. My mouth is dry and something sticky has dried on my face. Blood. They knocked me out. I'm stuck inside this stupid cell again by Vincent and his father. Why don't they kill me already? All this threatening and not doing anything gets old.

It doesn't matter. Nothing matters anymore. Why should I care? If Casper is dead, I want to be dead, too. I can't save the Elves. Not If the Jewel is linked to Vincent. The pain in my heart hits and as much as I don't want to cry, I can't help the tears that fall from my eyes. I don't have much fight in me. I miss Casper and I hate this so much. It isn't fair.

I have to try harder. If Casper is dead, it shouldn't affect my will to live. I've lived for him my entire life. If the last thing I do is to save his kind, then so be it. But I want to be free.

"Megan," I hear Vincent say.

Nausea hits my stomach and chills race up my spine. I hate the sound of his voice. I hate the way he says my name. I hate him.

"Yeah?"

"Why'd you take it from me? Knowing it would kill me."

I let out a sigh. "I wasn't trying to kill you. I...I wanted to get to the witch to end the spell on me. To end the curse on you. So we can be together." I tell him. Part of it is the truth. "King Jacques uses you and messes with you so much. Don't you see? I'm trying to save you."

As he moves into the small light, he looks less pale. He furrows his eyebrows. "What are you talking about? You poisoned me."

I look at him, pitying him. "I know. I knew you wouldn't let me go to the witch. You will never be happy if you don't stand up to your father. Ending the curse will make you a free man. Your father can no longer use you."

"You were taking the Jewel to the Elves."

"No, I was going to the witch. Why would I want to help them?" I rise to my feet, letting him see the tears on my face. "I love you, Vincent. Only you."

"What about Casper? I know you saw all the visions."

"I did. Casper compelled me. He only wanted the Jewel. I could tell he was trying to trick you when he talked about loving me. Though, I guess it kinda worked, since you killed him." I let out a small laugh.

"You're not upset?"

I cock my head to the side. "No. It was all fake. Maman told me everything you've done for them and me. I wish you had told me you're a dragon."

Darkness clouds his eyes. "I'm sorry. Even knowing all that, you're still not repulsed by me?"

I shake my head. "I have never been repulsed by you. I wish you trusted me. I know I broke your heart and I'm sorry. We've both done bad things to each other. That's what makes us *us*. I want to marry you. I want to be your queen. Your father has put doubt in you about me. You are not just a weapon, Vincent. You are so much more than that."

He says nothing.

"I never made you feel like you couldn't talk to me or share anything. I gave you everything. You say you love me but am I only a warm body to you? Don't you want me?"

He grabs my hands through the cell bars. "Of course, I love you. That's all I've ever wanted. You're my true love, Megan. You help me be a better person. Even in our previous human life, you helped me through so much. You're my everything."

I smile. "I am yours and you are mine."

"Do you want to run away with me?"

"Yes. We don't belong here. I don't want to die."

"I won't let the king kill you."

"How?"

"I will find a way." He kisses me through the cell bars, I still feel nothing. As long as he does, that's all that matters. He pulls back. "I will save you."

"And we'll go to the witch?"

"Yes. I've become such a crazed man, wrought with lust and rage." He peers into my eyes and I can see his pain and guilt. "You're right about everything. The king controls me and I've let him for far too long."

I shake my head. "No more apologies. Let's finally start anew."

"You really think the witch can save us both?"

"Only one way to find out. Either way, you'll be free of your father."

He releases a long sigh and walks away, leaving me to the silent darkness. I feel my lips stretch into a smile as I back into the wall. I slide down it and sit.

Once again, I'm left with memories of Casper, and I know I need to let go but I don't want to. Thinking of him is the only thing that keeps me sane. If I could see him one more time, I'd tell him how much I love him and how he changed my life. How I love him fiercely.

I will never see Casper again.

My heart falters at the thought, as it does every time it crosses my mind.

I inhale a deep breath. Vincent likes playing games. I can play, too. And I'll win. It's about time I get what I want. I will get out of this. Dead or alive, I will escape Vincent forever.

Sixteen

"Megan." I hear Vincent's voice as it yanks me from a light sleep. Sleep hasn't come easy, being in a cold, damp cell. The pain of losing Casper has taken ahold of me and refuses to release me. My muscles ache and I'm stiff and cold. I'm congested and my eyes are heavy.

"Vincent," I whisper.

He looks around like he's making sure no one followed him. Sweat rolls down his forehead as he fumbles with the keys. He unlocks the cell door, and it makes a loud whining noise as he opens it.

"We need to go."

I jump into his arms, wrapping mine around him and landing a kiss on his lips. He kisses me back with fervor.

"Come on. We have a small window."

I nod, taking his hand.

I felt brave last night. Now that bravery has vanished. I have to keep it up. Ignore the fear. I can do this.

Pulling me through the dark and dank tunnels of the underground, he follows a path like he's done numerous times. It's too dark and too quiet. I hear little squeaks every so often, which raises the hairs on the back of my neck. If I don't think about it, it's not real.

When we reach the end of a tunnel, he fumbles around until he finds a ladder. He climbs up the ladder and pushes open the heavy sewer door.

"Come on. It's the only way out so they won't see us."

I climb up the ladder, and he grabs my hand, helping me toward freedom.

I crawl upward and finally see daylight. It pushes me further and as I reach the soil of the earth; Vincent pulls me from the darkness.

A weight lifts from my soul, my body and I realize, I'm free.

Sort of.

Clasping onto Vincent's hand, we take off through dark woods of the village. Sparkling morning light dances between the coiling branches that dangle from the trees and an array of flowers, which has grown in abundance, adorn the amber backdrop.

Something doesn't feel right. I don't like Vincent's nervous energy or the paranoid way he keeps looking back. He is always confident. No matter what. I have never seen fear in his blue eyes. He's never run away before, or ever gone against his father's demands. A feeling deep inside tells me this isn't right. No good will come of this. I swallow hard, waiting for something to happen but nothing does.

"What if the King finds us?" he asks.

"They won't. We have to get out of here."

"What about the Elves?"

I never thought I would have to comfort him but here I am. At this point, he can run back to his precious daddy, and I'll keep going.

Vincent matches my pace. As I look ahead, I see soldiers. Defeat hits me in the chest and worms its way to my stomach.

Seventeen

Army Sprites surrounds us and one of them tackles me to the ground, my face scraping against the dry dirt. After he ties my hands behind my back, he lifts me to my feet. I look up to see King Jacques emerge from the group of men, a dark smile spreads across his lips.

"You can't be trusted, Megan. Trying to take my boy away."

"Father, it was my idea."

"The fact that you *still* believe this wench is beyond me. She's playing you. Where do you think you were going? To the Elves? As if they are your saviors. As if they will truly welcome you because you claim to love an Elf."

"Trying to end the curse, actually," I say to him. "Vincent deserves better than you."

He laughs. "And I'm sure you promised him better?" He lets out a sigh. "You have caused too much drama and you've broken my boy's heart too many times. You won't follow the rules. You have proven time and time again that you are a traitor, and you will continue to betray us. You are hereby sentenced to death by beheading."

Whatever strength I may have had vanishes. Tears fall as my chin quivers. A bulge lodges itself in my throat. I've lost everything. Death is my punishment for all I've done. It's the only way to survive.

"No! Father, you can't!" Vincent demands.

King Jacques cocks back his arm and plants his fist in Vincent's face. Down he goes, and I wince.

He holds his head high, as if he's proud he punched his son.

I stare into his eyes, hoping he can sense my animosity toward him. "Vincent's an Elf!" I shout and I'm met with laughter. "It's true. He and his father have been keeping it a secret. His mother is an Elf. He's been cursed as a dragon."

The soldiers laugh as Vincent looks at me like I've committed the ultimate betrayal. Part of me hates that I gave away his secret. No one believes me anyway. The King moves aside, and I see my father and mother. Disgrace clearly fills their eyes.

I gasp. Blood drains from my face.

"Why must you lie?" My father asks.

My mother collects tears with a handkerchief and shakes her head. "It's true. You ran away to be with *them*."

"Maman, please. I—"

She moves in front of me. Her blue eyes drowning in tears. "Tell me, mon enfant. Is it true you fell in love with an Elf? And ran away to be with him? That you were never compelled."

Looking at my weeping mother, I cannot lie to her. I never want to lie to her. "Please, you must understand they aren't who you think they are."

She gasps.

My father takes her by the shoulders. Disgust crosses his eyes.

"Maman—"

"You are no daughter of mine."

Tears cloud my vision as my parents turn their backs on me. They walk beside King Jacques. "No, Maman," I call but she ignores me. I've been gone so long I almost can't blame them for hating me. If only they knew the real reason, though I'm not sure they would even listen.

"Maman!"

The soldier jerks me against his body.

Blood runs down Vincent's nose as he makes his way toward me. "I can't believe you." He lifts my chin, forcing me to look at him. His eyes well with tears and I see fear. I know I've betrayed him and my people.

"I'm so sorry, Vincent." I am. I never meant to hurt him, my parents, or anyone.

"It didn't have to come to this. If only you had obeyed. You only care about yourself. It's always been about what you want."

"No, that's not true. They all need to know what they're fighting for. You can fight this."

An anguished look appears in his eyes. He presses his lips to me, showing me one final vision. It's of us, happily wed and watching our little ones run about in the fields. In that moment, I feel it. I feel the passion, the love, the want.

Vincent draws back slightly, and I press myself into him. "You can still be the better king," I whisper.

When he pulls away, the soldiers grab me and lead us to the main square of the village.

My heart lunges against my chest. I bite my lip as my stomach fills with nerves. I can't catch my breath and flashes of blue and white cloud my vision. I feel sick and without warning, I bend over as my stomach heaves out what little is inside. The guards jerk me up. Sweat collects around my face and I feel like I'm about to pass out.

As we reach the back of the village, people have gathered to watch me die. I pass by Jules and his daughter, Marie. Such a young child to be seeing this.

"Traitor!" the people yell.

A man spits on me as I walk past him. Someone throws mud in my face. The crowd grows chaotic. All the blood has drained from my face, I can feel it. I know I fled my home and my people, for who they assume is the enemy, but Vincent is the enemy. He and his father will always manipulate them.

"People of Château de Fées," I hear the King shout and I scan the crowd until I see him and Claudette overlooking us in a tower. "I know many of you deem me an unworthy King, but I never left you to be with the Elves."

The crowd boos.

"I never gave up my identity as a Sprite and I never will."

The crowd cheers.

"This woman has time and time again betrayed the Prince of the Sprites, her lover. Her own kind. She has betrayed you. She is a traitor who has tried putting us all in harm's way. She will die for these sins."

I can't look at the screaming crowd and I try my best to block out their uproars. My eyes land on Vincent, who stands next to his father. There is no emotion. There is no saving me. No one knows I'm in trouble. I cannot escape my fate and if I should die by a man who claims to love me, then so be it. I am too weak to fight him anymore. He will always win, no matter what.

The guards escort me up the stairs and place me in front of the chopping block. I lose my footing from the dizziness that overcomes me. I feel a little like Anne Boleyn. A man who claimed to have loved her, yet when she couldn't give him what he wanted, he told lies tarnishing her name and her image. She was beheaded for standing up for herself and trying to please her man.

As I brave a look into the crowd, my gaze sweeps over a woman about my age. She glares at me as she joins the rest of the taunts. She doesn't even know who I am, yet she hates me.

My heart pounds, deafening my ears, and bruising my chest. At least now, I will be free. Death always frees you. No one will miss me. They won't even know I'll be gone.

One of the men unties my wrists and once I see the sharp blade of the axe, nausea swims in my stomach again. Even though the people look at me in disgust and call me names, I stand proudly in front of them. Funny how a man can take so much from me, yet I still hold bits of pride.

The headsman nudges me to get on my knees. I ease down and take a deep breath before laying my neck across the block. The headsman moves my hair to the side. I refuse to cry. I will not give these people the satisfaction.

In the last moments of life, instead of looking at the cloudy day, or the muddy ground, I close my eyes and see his face. His beautiful blonde hair. The way he stares deeply at me before he kisses me. The way he tells me he loves me. The way his arms feel around me. It almost brings tears to my eyes. Soon, I will find him in death. I will be free of my misery and imprisonment.

I am ready.

A hush overcomes the crowd. Waiting.

Waiting for the blade to remove my head.

All I hear is the sound of my breath and the thumping of my heartbeat.

Waiting.

Eighteen

omeone screams. Gunshots fire. Then more screams. More gunshots. I open my eyes and see people scrambling from men holding guns. A man falls on me, his warm blood seeps into my clothes and I see his axe fall within inches of me.

Fear grips me. Has the crowd grown impatient? Are they trying to shoot me? Maybe if I stay here, they'll think I'm dead.

The sounds of the women, men, and children screaming is too much, even though these people want me dead. I can't listen to them anymore. I can't help them. I have to get out of here.

The heavy weight of the man disappears as someone picks me up.

"No!" I scream, struggling with their hands gripping me.

Fight! I tell myself. I kick and elbow the person. They fall.

Once I free myself, I see a girl lying on the ground, in danger of the advancing human stampede trampling her. Jumping off the stage, I snatch her arm, pulling her to her feet. We mix with the crowd, and I take her by the bushes near the stage. Blood runs down her face and is matted in her blonde hair. She shakes and cries yet gives me a baffling look. It's the same girl that I noticed moments before chaos ensued.

"You saved me," she says.

"I'm not your en—"

Hands grab me but I can't see who they are.

"You won't get away with this!" Vincent yells and as I turn, light flashes and all the chaotic sounds disappear. The man's arms wrap around me so tight and when I inhale, my heart pounds. The clean, woodsy scent fills my mind with memories of him, taunting me. My heart drops and I know I'm dreaming. This isn't real. That man beheaded me. I died on that podium, and this is my afterlife. We're both dead and our souls have reunited.

I grasp onto him like he is everything I have and kiss his neck.

As we slowly descend downward into a dark cave like we're floating, there is a blue hue around us. I'm not sure what it is but it's calming. I love the feeling of safety and fearlessness. Death is strange. Obscure.

When we land on solid ground, I hold onto him as tight as I can.

"It's okay, Megan," he says, and I don't want to release him or open my eyes to end the dream or whatever this is. He draws back slightly and lifts my chin. "Open your eyes."

I shake my head and warm tears fall. I feel his hands on both sides of my face. His thumbs wipe away my tears and dirt. I don't want this to end. I don't want him to vanish.

"Look at me please."

Inhaling, I slowly peel open my eyes. My heart melts when I see his beautiful brown eyes and I can't stop the sobs that escape me.

"Casper," I say. "No. No. No. You're dead. I saw it."

Without warning, he presses his lips to mine and my heart races. His lips are warm and soft as he kisses me with urgency, yet it's tender, like he wants to remember exactly how my lips feel against his. His hand grips my hair as he kisses me harder, and he groans. I feel him against me, and I feel the same fire and desire. I want him but now isn't the time. I feel everything when we kiss.

He pulls away, leaving us both breathless. I touch his chest and feel his beating heart. It's racing as fast as mine. I touch his face, his hair, his arm. It's real. All of this is real.

"I'm alive, Megan. I'm real."

I throw my arms around him, holding him as tight as I can.

"There is no amount of words that express how much I've missed you," he says, kissing me. "No words can describe this moment."

"I thought you were dead. I thought I would never see you again." My throat closes as more tears come.

"I'm here." He presses my head against his chest.

I inhale his scent deep inside letting it relax me.

"I'm dreaming. Or dead. They killed me."

"No, Megan, I promise, this is real."

"How did you…? When did you? How is this possible?"

Others begin to appear around us, and I bury my face in Casper's chest.

"It's okay," he says. "They're my friends. They helped me."

A tall Elf with long, white hair bows. He's older but still looks as though he's a fighter. "My lady."

"I'm no princess any longer."

"You will one day again. I'm Cyran. Known Casper since he was born."

"Pleasure to meet you."

Another tall man shakes my hand, his bright blue eyes appear kind yet strong. "I'm Silvyr. Casper's my oldest friend."

I meet Zev, a hulking man with a deep scar on his chin. He reminds me of one of those models on the cover of a romance novel, except his dark hair is short. He shakes my hand, and his eyes are still alive from the adrenaline. I can't imagine what I must look like. I wonder how Casper was able to convince them to save me. "It's so nice meeting you all but why would you risk your lives for me?"

"We're all in this together and Casper told us how important you are to him," Cyran says. "It wasn't that easy to decide."

"Plus, it gave us an excuse to attack the Sprites," Zev says.

Silvyr rolls his eyes and gives Zev a sidelong glance. "We're sorry for the barbaric way that had to happen."

Zev shrugs. "What? It was bound to happen."

"I didn't want a full panic for those people," Casper says. "Not all of them are evil."

"We should hurry back," Cyran says. "Vaelyn doesn't know we left."

"Vaelyn?" I ask.

"My mom," Casper says. "I will tell you everything, but we need to go."

I'm tired of running and I want to be done with fear and always on edge.

"I know," Casper says as if my face portrays my thoughts. He cradles my face. "It will be over soon, I promise. No more running. No more of any of this. I'm taking you home. We'll be safe there and we'll come up with a plan to end this war."

Home? Does he mean the mortal world or the Elf land? "They won't want me there."

"It'll be fine, I promise."

"I'm a Sprite."

"It's okay. I'll explain everything when we get there."

I nod. I have no doubt how much he wants to believe it. I can't help but feel he may be naïve.

He kisses me once more, igniting my heart. He takes my hand and I love how smooth and warm his skin is next to mine. The five of us follow a path in the tunnel with the mysterious blue light all around us. I don't hear the sounds of war and I realize how quiet it is.

Silence is a wonderful thing after months of loud noises, screams, and chaos.

"Where is the light coming from?" I ask.

"The orb. We're traveling in one."

"An orb? I didn't think they existed." I also didn't think dragons were real either. Orbs were a way of travel by some Elves, though they don't work like the Jewel. It can be used to travel so many miles, but it doesn't allow travel to different worlds.

"We've kept a lot of things secret." Zev winks at me.

We walk along in the strange orb. It's like a bubble of light that shrouds us as we move. It's incredible.

I squeeze Casper's hand, loving the smooth feel of it, loving that he's here with me. Alive. There is so much that I need to tell him but for once, I want to enjoy the moment with him. Even if we're not alone. It doesn't matter. The adrenaline, fear, and stress begin to fade away, leaving me with exhaustion.

Casper squeezes back. "It's not much further."

I nod.

"I can't believe you're here with me. I've longed for this day since we were parted."

"How did you survive that fall over the cliff?"

Casper sets his jaw. "I washed up on the shore. I was lucky I didn't hit any rocks. By the time I woke, you two were long gone. After several weeks, I found my way home and explained everything to my friends. It wasn't easy convincing my mother to rescue you and that's why we left without her knowing."

"I can't imagine what you went through. How did you know where I was or that I was in trouble?"

"After I explained everything, several of us secretly returned to the Sprite kingdom, like Edmond and I did before. We blended in and heard all the villagers talk about how the King planned to behead you. It had been days, and no one had seen you. Until that day in the square. Seeing you on that stage *killed* me. I had to do whatever it took. We weren't supposed to shoot any guns or definitely cause a panic, but I freaked out once I saw you."

A tear escapes down my cheek. "Vincent showed me a vision of you exchanging me for the Jewel. You handed me over like you never loved me."

He stops us and frowns. "It was a trick. He shot me." He pulls me into an embrace. His arms warm around me, swallowing me in his safety. We've both been through hell and here we are together, stronger than ever. Our love will strengthen us, as it always has. Yet that strange, empty feeling is still there. I don't know what it is or how to get rid of it.

He starts walking but I stop him while the others keep moving ahead of us.

"Casper, there's something I need to tell you."

"What is it?"

"Vincent. He's...part Elf and...he's a dragon."

"What? Is this more of his lies?"

I shake my head. "No. I've seen it."

His eyes widen. "What?"

"I stole the Nuummite and I saw things."

"What kind of things?"

"It was like I witnessed his memories. I saw him throw you over the cliff like it was nothing. I saw him talk to his father about me, about how he had to marry me or give me up. In a couple of the visions, I felt like I was a dragon flying over but it was Vincent's thoughts."

"How were you able to see or feel those things?"

"It's the Jewel. It has to be. Vincent's connected to it, Casper. He has to keep it, or he'll die."

"What happened? Did they catch you with it?"

"The strangest thing came over me. It felt like it was possessing me almost, or strongly encouraging me to return it to Vincent. It started making me believe that the Jewel belonged to the Sprites. I couldn't fight it."

We continue walking. He's quiet. His silence doesn't bother me because I know he's thinking. I missed the peacefulness about him, his calming effect. I can't believe he's here. I know I have to be dreaming, because I've wanted this for so long and after believing he never loved me to believing he died, my heart can't take much more.

I squeeze his hand letting him know I'm here for him. He squeezes back. I missed the tranquil peace I feel when I'm with Casper. It's like my worries fade with him because no matter what, he's always there for me.

When we reach the end of the tunnel, Casper takes me in his arms and within seconds, we're all in another tunnel weaving through the undergrounds. Once we arrive at the end, the orb transports us to a place harrowed by war. It reminds me of the land where I found the cottage and the unfortunate body inside. Dead trees lay everywhere, though luckily there aren't any dead bodies. There isn't a single sound, as though the forest animals died.

"I've seen so much death and destruction," I say.

"I know. I know this hasn't been easy for you. I can't imagine what all you've gone through, but I promise it'll get better. It won't be like this forever."

I nod, not feeling strong right now.

The deeper we walk into the desolate forest, the more it begins to change. I see vibrant greens in the trees, the flowers, the ground. The longer we walk, the more the land looks untouched by war. It's beautiful and unlike anything I've seen. I've never seen such colors in real life. Once we clear the forest, I see mountains reaching incredibly high, past the clouds with several cascading waterfalls. The vast mountain range fades into the horizon. The air smells clean and fresh with a hint of evergreen. It feels cooler here and I'm sure it's from the lush thick forest providing abundant shade.

There is a river that cuts through the land, sparkling beneath the golden sun. Birds chirp happily as they fly from one tree to another. Scurrying animals play in the shrubs.

As the sun sets, the colors of the forest seem to glow. Luminescent and brilliant pinks and blues and oranges and greens from exotic plants that I've never seen. Several shades of red, yellow, pink, white come alive from lily, hibiscus, rose, and several other plants. I've never seen so much color in my life.

Off in the distance, I see a castle and buildings resting on the edges of cliffs from the mountains. The city is beautiful.

"*This* is where you're from?" I ask.

"Yes. Welcome to Belle Palais."

"Quite the opposite of what you're used to, I'd say," Zev says.

"It's beautiful." As I walk through, I'm in awe of the intense beauty. It feels unreal. Like a dream. I wince. I can't help but feel like none of this is real. Maybe in a day or two, it will. Whatever it is, I want to enjoy it for as long as I possibly can.

"We'll meet up with you later," Cyran says. "Perhaps I'll find Vaelyn and calm her fears before she panics when she sees Megan."

Casper nods. "Thank you for helping."

"You never have to thank us," Silvyr says.

"Thank you for saving my life," I tell them. "I owe you all."

Cyran bows his head. "If all the Sprites were as warm and lovely as you, none of us would be at war. Welcome to Belle Palais."

The three of them walk away and Casper moves in front of me with a crooked smile and I love it. I missed it. "Come with me."

"Where? Don't we need to talk to your mom and the Elves?"

"Give me a moment. I need a moment with you."

His lips meet mine and he lifts me up as my legs wind around his waist. I feel my back gently press against a tree trunk. He moans as his hands wander across my body. Casper deepens the kiss and it's everything I need. Everything I want. Heat washes over me as my pulse climbs higher and higher. It's been too long that we lose ourselves in our feverish kisses. No dream could ever make me feel like this.

Casper eases me onto my feet and leaves feather-like kisses across my face. "I love you, Megan."

"I love you."

He lifts a corner of his mouth. "I needed that."

I return the smile. "Me, too."

"I promised myself I would find my way back to you. That I will do whatever I can to save you. That I will make it safe for us, that we will never have to live in fear again. You never deserved what Vincent did to you. You are an amazing, beautiful woman and I'm sorry he treated you so horribly. You are safe now."

Tears blur my vision, but I push them away. I'm tired of hearing that. Can't I decide if I'm safe or not? Does everyone think they know what's best for me?

Taking my hand, he leads me deeper into the woods and slows when we reach the edge of the ocean. I see faint pink lights glowing right below the surface.

As I move forward to step into the water, he stops me, pulling me down the shore to a dock. As we climb on top, I see people walking toward us.

"Casper." I squeeze his hand.

"It's okay. Most nights we come to watch this." He points to the water. I watch as floating lights make their way to the surface. "They're moon jellyfish. They come out each night dancing right beneath the surface."

"It's amazing."

"When I saw you that night at prom, I had to do a double-take. You have always been gorgeous but seeing you that night." He shakes his head. "It was like the breath had been knocked out of me. I knew then how much I love you and that I had to tell you. But I couldn't be selfish with you. I had to let you be happy with whatever you chose. Your eyes told me one thing, but you told me something completely different.

"After you left, I was scared that I had lost you. I felt defeated and helpless. I've been out here every night hoping and praying I hadn't lost you." He takes my hand. "And here you are." He leans down, pressing his lips to mine. In that moment, I feel safe and at peace. There's not a single worry in my mind and heart. I'm happy and it feels great. It's something I've only felt since Casper has come into my life. It's the most remarkable feeling.

Seeing all the jellyfish floating, alive with colors, makes me think of them as all the lives Casper and I ever had. There were so many, and we were happy in all of them. In all our lives together, I love this one the most because it's real. After every heartache, battle, happiness, this is the truest because at any moment we could die and never be reborn. This life counts and my love for Casper is the strongest. In this life, nothing can be taken for granted.

When Casper pulls away, he holds me, and we watch the jellyfish dance in the moonlight. We both relax, if only for a night. It's all I've ever wanted. There's still that nagging feeling inside me. In no lifetime, will Casper and I truly be happy unless the war is over, and Vincent is dead.

Nineteen

nce the jellyfish fade into the darkness, Casper and I turn around. I gasp when I see hundreds of Elves across the shore and the docks. I squeeze Casper's hand, not knowing what to do.

"Casper!" a woman cries from the crowd and runs toward him. She looks a lot like Casper but older. She has the same brown eyes, same blonde hair except hers is much longer. She grabs him, pulling him into a hug and weeps.

"I'm fine, Mom."

I feel a twinge of sadness as I watch them embrace. I will never get to feel that ever again. My parents turned their backs on me, letting Vincent and his father manipulate them and everyone else. I look away, letting them have their moment, privately.

Suddenly, I feel nervous. I've never met his mother and I'm the reason he hasn't seen her in several years, with the exception of the small amount of time he came here to gather a group of Elves to come save me. I look down at my clothes. I'm still wearing some strange man's clothes and I'm covered in dirt. I know I must smell, and my hair is probably matted with terrible tangles. His mother is about to meet the woman he risked his life for and she's disgusting.

When they pull apart, Casper turns to me with a smile that's all teeth. "Mom, this is Megan. Megan, this is my mom, Vaelyn."

She covers her mouth and tears fall from the corners of her eyes. "She's beautiful. It's so nice to finally meet you."

My heart falters. "You as well," I say taking her hand.

"I know you're both exhausted and need rest," she says. "Please, let's eat and rest. Casper can regale us with his heroic tale of saving you." She smiles but something seems amiss about the way she looks at me. I don't know if I'm paranoid, since I'm the only Sprite in this entire land of Elves, or if she has some ill will toward me. I sense it.

"Mom, we need to speak to the council. Tonight. This isn't over."

"I'm sure it isn't," she says, her eyes glancing over me. "Not when she's here."

"I'm afraid this is bigger than just me," I say, and swallow a hard lump. Her eyes turn dark, forcing me to look away.

"Perhaps you two should clean up then we will talk. You've both had a rough and long journey."

The thought of taking a shower warms my heart. I don't even know the last time I took one, with the exception of the storm I ran through.

"Okay," Casper says.

She nods and walks away as her court people follow her.

"So, you're the Sprite who's caused all this fighting." A woman with smooth, golden-brown skin approaches us. Long, dark tendrils fall to her waist. Her green eyes rove over me and I can't decide if her disgust is from my appearance or because I'm a Sprite. The way she looks at me reminds me of Amber. Seems like a lifetime ago since she terrorized me.

"Hi Casper." She smiles at him like there's a secret between them and I hate the jealous feeling that rises inside me.

"Saida." He nods, barely meeting her eyes. I don't know her or their history but there seems to be one.

"I'm glad you're okay and didn't die while saving her."

I swallow hard, feeling uncomfortable. No one wants me here. Why did I come? I don't belong here. I fell in love with an Elf, and I am outcast from my own home and now here. They don't want me here and I'm not sure Casper sees it. He could be happy with Saida. They are both Elves and they will have Elf children.

I should leave. I want to go home. Will Casper come with me though?

"I'm fine, Saida," he says.

"I know. It's good to see you. I've missed you." She hugs him and he returns the hug. I don't like how tight her arms wind around him.

I don't want to be here. I haven't felt much happiness lately. People don't like me and if they want me, it's only because they need something. They don't really need me though. I will never be someone's number one priority. There will always be someone else, never me. I don't understand why I'm having these thoughts. Casper just risked his life for me. Maybe I'm tired.

They pull apart and Saida smiles at me like she won something. I look away. I need to rest.

Casper takes my hand, and we follow the crowd toward the castle.

As we walk through the forest outside of the castle gates, I'm still amazed by all the brilliant colors light up by bioluminescent creatures. Like the glowing jellyfish and oddly enough, even the flowers glow.

Casper holds my hand and chuckles.

"What?"

"You're smiling and your face is lit up. I love seeing it. It makes me happy, and I missed it."

I smile, letting the warm feeling fill me. I take a deep breath and let myself relax, if only for a little while.

We approach a set of metal gates covered with greenery and purple flowers like wisteria vines that snake their way in and out and around. At the sight of Casper's mother, the guards step aside. We follow her through, and I inhale the sweet floral scent. The castle has clearly stood the test of time. Several thick, square towers dominate the skyline of this massive castle and are connected by towering, thin walls made of dark brown stone. Stylish windows are scattered here and there around the walls in fairly symmetrical patterns.

Everything is hidden, like some secret in the forest. The land is greener, lusher. The people also look happier and less like they're under control of a maniacal person.

Casper takes my hand, leading me through the beautiful, ornate castle. It's not at all similar to the palace I grew up in but it's as beautiful and intricately designed. Paintings of gardens, flowers and Elves decorate the walls. Everything is way more modern than the Sprite palace. Fresh flowers are placed in vases along the walls filling the halls with sweet, fragrant scents.

It takes a second to realize why so many of the Elves stare at me. I'm different than them and it definitely feels that way. I don't like being the center of attention especially when it's negative. I know Casper notices, but he carries on like a proud man with a normal girl on his arm.

I don't know how he's able to maintain his confidence. Mine is breaking with every step inside the Elf castle. Maybe Vincent was right. If Casper weren't here, they would eat me alive.

Trying to ignore them, we finally make it to his room. It's a huge room with large windows to brighten it. The windows overlook the amazing colorful, sparkling forest. I'm amazed at the openness and how enormous it is. A king size bed is against the wall and a matching chest is across from it.

Once Casper closes the door, he turns to me, pulling me to him, hard. He holds me, and I breathe in his scent. "I missed you so much. I can't tell you how happy I am that you are here."

"I missed you."

My nerves are shot, and I don't want to talk about anything. Not tonight. I want to be in his arms, feel his touch. I need him. I want him. I want to forget the last several months or however long it's been. I want to be with him in this moment.

He tugs me toward the shower, which is impressive. Black and white marble countertops and large mirrors. It feels modern. Unlike anything I've seen in this world. The Elves haven't been living in the past. It's still not as upgraded as the human world but it's so much better than the Sprites. Belle Palais has been its own world for centuries and I can imagine now why the Sprites want to overtake it. I hope they never destroy this beautiful world.

"Not expecting this?"

"Not at all. The Sprites are still living in the eighteenth century."

"You never have to return. I want to show you how much I love you. Only if you're ready."

"I'm ready. I've been ready."

A smile tugs at the corner of his mouth. "I can't believe you're here, Megan."

"Me either. I've wished for this for so long. I always knew I loved you, even in my human life. Even when I fought against it. It was too strong, and I knew Vincent was no good for me. It's always been you, Casper. It always will be."

Turning on the water, he turns to me. "Are you sure?" he asks.

"Yes." He presses his lips to mine, slipping his tongue past. Heat pours over me, and I remove his shirt. Our kiss turns frantic and urgent. It doesn't matter how many times, how many centuries we've kissed, it always feels exciting and new. His hand tangles in my hair. Eagerness thrums through my veins. The gentle way his fingers trace underneath my shirt sends shivers curling down my spine.

Casper removes my shirt and my pants. He carries me into the shower and kisses me hard as the warm water pelts us. His lips slip over mine and he holds me so close to his body. It's Casper and me. No one else. No war. Nothing.

Just us exploring each other.

Twenty

When I wake the next day, it takes me a second to remember that I'm in Casper's room, enfolded in his arms. I twist my head and watch him peacefully sleep. I trace his bare chest and his stomach flinches as I hit a ticklish spot. I reach further until he moans. He slowly opens his eyes and stares at me with lust.

"Good morning." He smiles. "Did you sleep well?"

"Good morning. I did. How long did we sleep?"

"A while. It's afternoon."

My hand rakes through his hair and he leans in, kissing me. His lips travel over my neck, across my collarbone as his hand grips my hip. Heat rises as my pulse quickens. In a quick motion, he moves on top of me and once again, I revel in the warmth, love, and intense emotions that we share.

We dress, after Casper fetched a few items of clothing for me. One is a simple white, cotton dress. It feels amazing to have showered, slept in a bed, and wear clean clothes with no corsets.

"I know we need to tell the Elves everything, but I want one day with you," Casper says. "Without the war. Drama. I haven't seen you in months and we've not had that since before we were human. I want to show you all these things in case there never will be a time."

"Don't speak like that."

"I know but Vincent could easily turn into the dragon and burn this place to the ground."

"He could." But he wouldn't. At least if he stands up to his father like I know he can.

"Just one day."

I want that, too. Even though I need to talk to him about returning to the human world, the pleading look in his eyes makes me agree. "Okay." Maybe this is what I need to erase the emptiness.

Casper takes my hand, leading me downstairs and I take in the beauty of the castle with fresh eyes. The cathedral ceiling is arched with intricate gold architecture for support. Beautiful mosaics of trees, flowers, animals are splayed across the walls and ceilings in brilliant colors. As we make our way down a long hallway, the sun hits them perfectly and it feels like walking through a corridor of lights.

"Casper?"

We stop and turn to face his mother, Vaelyn.

"Good morning," she says. "You really are beautiful."

"Thank you." I don't feel beautiful. Elves stare at me, and I can feel their loathing emanating. I'm also still tired from stress, emotions, the pending war.

"After breakfast, we should meet," Vaelyn says.

"I have plans for Megan today."

Vaelyn lowers her head. "Casper, you cannot parade her around. Not everyone knows she is here, including the Queen."

I swallow hard. The Queen doesn't know that I'm here.

"Then maybe she should," Casper says. "Megan is a part of us. She's on our side."

Vaelyn presses her lips in a tight line. "It isn't that easy, you know this. It's too risky."

He shakes his head. "One day. Everything will be fine."

"Casper, do not be foolish."

He tilts his head and takes her hands in his. "I promise, we will be careful. We'll meet with you tomorrow." He kisses her cheek before he turns around, pulling me with him.

"Casper, maybe we should talk to her."

"Not today."

"Why doesn't the Queen know I'm here? I thought you said it was okay that I'm here. Don't we need to tell everyone the truth of the Jewel?"

He hesitates. "She doesn't know we saved you. A lot of the Elves still see you as an enemy."

My jaw drops. "How could you do that? This could have you killed. Or me."

He cradles my face in his hands. "I won't let that happen. I have to tell the Queen my story. She'll understand."

"Then, what are we doing? Shouldn't we go to her now?"

"It's okay. I promise. One day."

"Casper." I warn.

"We will talk to her. We both need this before anything else happens."

"Are you sure?"

"Yes."

I don't understand his urgency for this, but I reluctantly agree. There is so much to talk about. So much to tell the Queen. I trust him and I know he'd never put me in harm's way. Even though I'm a secret living among the Elves. So many have already seen me. He seems so confident but there is something bothering him. I just can't tell what.

Once we reach the outdoors, I'm once again in awe of the lush colors of the palace. The sun warms me. The slight breeze in the air sends a salty ocean scent. I love the ocean, and the closer we move toward it, the faster my heart beats.

As we continue walking through the sublime beauty of the Belle Palais, Casper slides his hand in mine, and I relax. We reach the docks, and he helps me into a small rowboat. He gets in and unties the rope from the dock. Holding out his hand, he helps me into the small boat.

As we row across the shallow part of the ocean, I watch him. Every time he pulls the boat, his muscles flex and I can't help but feel warm all over. The way he concentrates to row us against the current is mesmerizing to watch.

Soon we begin to approach caves, and as he rows underneath, the temperature cools the moment. It's dark but glowing lights from the plants provide enough light for us. The ceiling glitters with twinkling little blue lights.

"Those are fireflies," he says. "They stay in here during the day."

There are even lights glowing from beneath the surface of the water. It's like out of a movie or something.

"I know I keep saying this, but this is so beautiful. You've lived here your whole life. Why did you want to leave ages ago?"

"I had to find the Jewel. The Queen ordered a group of us to go undercover to find the Jewel, so we did. Honestly, I'm not sure how we managed to get away with it. Sort of. Then I met you."

I smile.

"I gave up on trying to find the Jewel because nothing is worth more than you." He stops rowing so that we're floating along the twinkling of the cave. I'll always remember this moment with him.

"When I met you, it felt like time stopped and as we got to know each other, I knew you were more than special. You have my heart and always will. You make me the happiest I've ever been. I never knew such happiness until you. You're unique, caring, strong, and beautiful. I love the day we met and every life we've shared. I want to share the rest of our lives together. Megan, will you marry me?"

I gasp as he holds out a ring for me. White gold weaves an intricate design holding a round diamond in the center. It sparkles under the glowing lights, and I can feel the tears and emotion lodging inside my throat. "Yes!"

Before he can pull the ring out of its holder, I practically tackle him and kiss him. I love the warmth of his lips on mine and the way his arms wrap around me. I love the way I feel when I'm with him and it's like I can't get enough. He is the best thing that has ever happened to me. My love for him grows each second.

Casper pulls away from the intense kiss and slides the ring on my finger. It feels amazing and I want this feeling to last forever.

We spend the day drifting along the path of water through the tunnels in each other's arms. It's beautiful and relaxing. Still, something is off with him, and I can't figure it out. I know he's happy, but I can sense sadness or something. By the time we return the boat to the dock, the sun is setting.

"Casper, this whole day has been beautiful and wonderful."

He squeezes my hand, smiling. "It has. I can tell you're struggling with something, though."

I've never been able to hide anything from him. I swallow hard. "Ever since I've been back to Arvada, I've had this…empty, weird feeling inside me. I thought maybe it was because I was with Vincent and everything happening there. After spending the day with you, I'm so happy and I want to spend the rest of my life with you but that feeling is still there. It isn't as strong though. I don't know what it is."

"Maybe it's all the things you've been through. You're trying to heal and you're trying to get back to normalcy. It'll take time though. It's been so long since we've been back. Plus, everything is so different for you."

"Maybe. I know there's more. I can't stop thinking about our human life. I've been wanting to return to the mortal world."

"What? Why?"

"I feel so drawn to it, like I can't let it go. It's so powerful."

"We did spend a lot of time there. Maybe you got so used to life there."

I shrug. "What about you?"

He shakes his head. "No, I don't feel anything for it. All I feel is relief because you're standing here and we're together," he says, but something is off about the way he says it. He seems sad. There has been a sort of sadness all day with him.

Nodding, I take his hands. "Why the urgency today? Why are you acting like it's the last time I'm going to see you?"

Uncertainty is written all over the lines in his face. "I was hoping I could hide that better."

My heart stills. "What is it?"

"Megan, this war won't go away, and I have to be a part of it. It has to stop."

"You're leaving me to go fight?"

"I have to. I will find Vincent and kill him."

"You can't kill him. The second he sees you he will kill you. He won't hesitate."

"I know this. He's already tried."

"Exactly. It's too dangerous for you."

"He's stronger than most Elves. If we get enough involved—"

I shake my head. "No. He's not the one we need to kill."

"What?" His eyes widen. "You're joking, right? He sent you to your death or did you forget?"

"It wasn't him. He freed me. His father controls him. He wouldn't have let me die in those gallows. He was willing to run away with me."

Casper drops my hand. "Are you defending him?"

"What? No."

"Have you forgotten everything he's done?"

"No, I haven't, but who are we to decide if someone should live or die? We'd be as bad as him and his father. Both our sides have been at war for years because of Vincent. We have to convince the Elves to end the curse. If he becomes a dragon, he will slaughter everyone."

Casper sighs and runs his hands through his hair. "I can't believe what you're saying. Has he manipulated you?"

Anger rises in me. "No one has manipulated me. No one has compelled me. I love you, Casper. I messed with Vincent so that I could escape that place. I thought you were dead, and I thought I had nowhere to go. I wanted Vincent and me to find the witch to end his curse and so she could return me to the mortal world. That's the truth. Vincent doesn't deserve to die. He's a boy abused by his father. A father who's using him as a weapon."

I don't want to fight with Casper, especially on the same day we became engaged. No matter how much Vincent's done, I don't want him to die. I would never wish anyone's death. Does that make me a bad person? Does that make me weak? I can't be the reason for the deaths of so many people anymore and if we can break the curse, then we'll all be free.

Twenty-One

I wander around Casper's room, trying to calm my nerves. I didn't mean to blow up on him, and right now, I need some time to myself. The room smells like him. There are small pictures of us smiling, kissing, completely in love. I wonder if he grabbed these from the human world.

We're going to talk to his mother tonight. I can already tell she doesn't like me. It could be that Casper is keeping me a secret which could potentially endanger both of us. Everything is so messed up and the only thought that keeps popping in my head to fix it is to return to my human life.

I can't leave Casper. I won't leave Casper. I want him with me.

Someone knocks on the door, and it opens. Tall, slim, and beautiful in a flowy orange dress, Saida enters. Her long hair has been curled and covers her smooth shoulders. The little gold specks in her green eyes are quite prominent. Her features may be small but they're dramatic. High cheekbones. Perfect eyebrows that crown her eyes.

"Good evening," she says.

"Hello," I say, wondering why she's in here.

"Such a beautiful Sprite. I've never seen one so close." She walks up to me, staring. Her eyes rove over me as if she's judging me. She's not afraid of me and I can see the curiosity.

Saida exudes confidence as if she has nothing to worry about. "Perhaps one day, you and I will become the best of friends. I am a little concerned with some of the people here. They don't necessarily want you here. I feel like you will need protection."

I roll my eyes. Do I have a sign on my forehead that screams I need protection? "Are you going to provide that?"

"No. I can help though. You must know that no one wants you here. Bringing you here only leads the Sprites right to us. Casper must have known that. Makes me think that was why he brought you here." She looks away, pursing her lips as in thought.

Her words slam into me and weighs on my heart. "That isn't the only reason."

"Oh, of course not, my dear," she says as she takes my arm in hers. "Casper adores you. He did save you after all."

"He also proposed." I hold up my hand, showing her the ring.

She gasps, looking worried, then quickly recovers with a smile. "How wonderful!"

"Thanks. Is there anything you needed? I'm waiting for Casper to return for dinner."

"Oh, you can come with me."

I'm not sure if I should trust her. I can't read her well. "Sure."

"Great." With a sly smile, she walks toward the door, opening it.

I don't want to go to dinner with her, but I need to make friends. It's clear no one is that pleased that I'm here.

I follow her out the door, and she leads me to a large common room where several Elves are eating. She hooks her arm with mine and as we pass, the stares continue. It's almost as if I'm naked. I hate it.

"If they see that I'm friends with you, it won't be so bad," she says. "I know we don't know each other well, but I trust Casper. He has good intuitions. A lot of people question him now that he's with you and since he's risked so much for you."

"I never asked him to do that."

"Of course not, dear."

"This war involves all of us. Not just the Elves."

Saida removes her arm from mine and shifts in front of me. Her eyes glare into mine, yet she holds a smile on her face. I hold my ground. "The *Sprites* started this war, and we will finish it. Don't forget that."

Squaring my shoulders, I place my hands on my hips. "Don't forget that we're on the same side."

She smirks. "Only because the Sprites no longer want you. Didn't your parents turn against you, as well?"

My heart sinks as her words cut deep. Casper told her? How could he? "You want my help or not?"

"You have no choice but to help us. You've nowhere to go, Megan."

Actually, there is somewhere I can go. "There is so much you know nothing about and without me, you may never find out."

Saida lifts an eyebrow. "You'd be surprised at what I can find out."

"What's going on?" Casper asks from behind me, and I relax. "I see Saida brought you to dinner. I came to get you."

"Yeah, but I'm no longer hungry."

"What's wrong," he asks. I want to be alone with him. I'm not ready for all these people and trying to prove myself to them. I spent so much time by myself I almost don't know how to act anymore around people. I don't belong here. I am the enemy in their eyes. I am dangerous to them.

"She's probably still tired," Saida says. "She's had a rough time. Perhaps you two should spend some time together." She leans forward. "Also, congratulations, though I'm not sure it's the right time for that."

I can't figure her out. Is she my friend or enemy? Only friendly when Casper's present. It's been a while since I've been around people that I'm so out of touch.

Casper shakes his head with disappointment in his eyes as he stares at Saida. "It doesn't matter what you think."

She raises an eyebrow. "No but the rest of the Elves aren't going to like this, Casper."

"Megan is with us now. I love her and I intend to be with her. I don't care if it's not the right time. If anything, it's the perfect time." He turns to me. "Let's eat."

I nod. "Okay." I let him lead us to a table and as soon as we sit, the three Elves who were sitting, get up and leave. I love him for standing up for me but it's making things worse for him. For me. They all seem to think I'm controlling him.

"It's not you," he says. I know he's just trying to make me feel better.

"It *is* me and they won't give me the time of day until I prove myself to them."

He narrows his eyes. "You don't have to prove anything."

"Yes, I do. They hate me here."

"They don't know you."

"You don't see it?"

"I don't care."

His response irritates me. How can he not care? "Well maybe I do. I'm not like you. I can't just let things roll off my chest like it's nothing." I hate that we keep fighting. It isn't like us.

"It's not that it doesn't bother me. I just can't worry about what they think. They will have to get used to it because we're together."

I look away, crossing my arms in front of my chest.

He exhales. "I'm sorry. I'm only trying to play my cards right. If I act afraid, then everyone else will act worse. I love you, Megan. I've got your back no matter what. I need to know is this what you want? You mentioned returning to the human world."

I uncross my arms and meet his heavy gaze. "You are what I want." I lean over and his lips touch mine.

Being in this place isn't what I want though. Maybe it'll get better with time.

Twenty-Two

The nerves in my stomach prevent me from eating much of the delicious roast and vegetables. The food is very rich, especially after barely eating the last several weeks. Once we finish, Casper and I make our way to see his mother. Clasping his hand tightly in mine, I'm sure he can tell my palms are sweaty. My pulse races and warmth swathes my entire body making me lightheaded. There's a terrible taste in my mouth and I wish I had water or something.

I don't want to talk to his mother. I don't want to have to explain everything to a bunch of people who won't listen or care. No way will they believe me.

When we enter a parlor, I glance around the room, barely noticing the three chandeliers hanging from a vaulted ceiling. While the room is dim, I can see the hard look in Vaelyn's eyes and her tightly pressed lips. She sits in a chair toward the center of the room, gripping its arms. Saida stands nearby with a half-smile as other Elves line the wall. I recognize Cyran, Silvyr, and Zev among them.

"Engaged?" Vaelyn says. Her voice is full of discontent. "Casper, you know as well as I do this can't happen."

My throat tightens and I feel sick.

Casper squeezes my hand. "I love her, and it will happen. That isn't why we're here."

"I am so disappointed in you. She is supposed to be a secret. Now, this entire village knows about her."

"Why should I be kept a secret?" I ask, knowing the answer. "Several Elves have seen me already."

Vaelyn snaps her eyes to me, and I immediately regret speaking. "We have small groups of Elves, but we've all been sworn to secrecy from telling the Queen that you are here. If she finds out we helped a Sprite, we will all be punished."

"You live in the castle. Don't you think she'll see me?"

Saida snickers. "The Queen lives in her own castle. Belle Palais is a lot larger than what you're used to."

Casper lets out a sigh. "She can't be a secret. We must see the Queen. Megan knows things that we need to tell her."

"What things?"

He urges me to start.

I clear my throat. "Um. Well. Ever since I was a small child, I always thought the story of the dragon was a fairytale. I'm here to say, the dragon is real. His name is Vincent and he's a Sprite. Also, an Elf. The Nuummite Jewel is to keep him a human. It isn't to keep the Elves from aging quickly. It isn't to keep the Sprites safe, either."

A mixture of gasps and laughter fill the room.

"What?" Casper looks to me. "Are you certain? If the Jewel isn't to keep us from aging, then why have we been at war all these years?"

Vaelyn raises her hand to silence us. "That is ridiculous."

Cyran crosses his arms in front of his chest. "Let her speak."

"The war is because of King Jacques and an Elf. She abandoned Vincent as a baby, then cursed him. The Elves and Sprites were told lies about the Jewel to keep the mixed baby a secret. King Jacques is set on using Vincent as a weapon."

"This is preposterous," Vaelyn says.

The tension in the room gushes in like a broken water pipe. I take comfort knowing I'm not the only one who has been in the dark about the truth.

"I know I'm certain. As much as I can't stand Vincent, I know he's been honest with me. I've seen it. Think about it, the Sprites have had the Jewel for centuries and it hasn't affected the Elves."

"I beg to differ," Vaelyn scoffs. "The Sprites have almost wiped us out several times. We need the Jewel to keep us safe. Many of us are aging at a very fast—"

"But you're not, are you?" I ask, challenging her. "You've been fighting the Sprites for so long. The Jewel does nothing but keep the dragons in their human form."

She shakes her head. "I will not have some stranger, let alone some insignificant *Sprite*, speak to me this way. I will hear no more of this nonsense. What are you trying to gain by speaking such lies?"

"Mom—"

"I mean no disrespect, but I am not lying."

"You're a Sprite. That's all you do, and you've dragged my son into your dangerous web."

"Vaelyn," Cyran warns.

I'm shocked, which I expected this. Did Vincent lie to me? Have I fallen into yet another trap of his? I have to remind myself that this isn't one of his traps. I've seen the dragon. I saw what it did to Vincent not having it. I also saw his father's obsession with it. I have to convince them. Otherwise, they will kill me or use me. "It's true. I assure you."

Vaelyn moves closer to me and Casper flinches. "There are no dragons, dear. There haven't been for many centuries. You are only trying to convince my son and other Elves to lay down their swords so the Sprites will take over. You certainly have no say in the matter because you have been gone for years. You have no idea what's been happening."

"Is this why you didn't want us to find her?" Casper asks.

"My son, I'm sorry that this woman has tricked you."

"You don't know what you're talking about."

"I never wanted you to find her because she's done nothing but hurt you. You wouldn't have almost died several times had it not been for her." Her chin quivers for a second, then she recovers. "But now that she is here, perhaps she can be useful. She is key in this war. She can give us insights to the Sprites and tell us how to take them down. If she doesn't, we will torture her."

Casper moves quickly in front of me. "You will not hurt her."

Vaelyn narrows her eyes at him, and I hate that I've caused this.

"No, stop." I move out from behind Casper. "Together, we can stop the war. I will help however I can. I love your son with all my heart. I can't do this without him."

"My son has risked his life too many times to save you. You do *not* deserve him."

"Mom, how can you say that?"

"I will not listen—"

"No, you listen. You don't know the hell she has been through. She has saved me several times, and she loves me. Megan has suffered far too much abuse and torture because of that love. The dragon is real. I've seen it. So, either you start telling us the truth or the truth will find you."

He's seen the dragon? He never mentioned it before.

Vaelyn takes a deep breath, staring at her son like he's a stranger.

"I've seen it too," Zev says. "It's as black as midnight and mysterious. I wasn't sure it was a dragon at first, but I saw it again."

"Are you certain?" Saida asks as her eyes widen.

"Thought it was a bad dream. No, it was real."

Vaelyn shakes her head. "None of this is real. You all dreamed such occurrences. This beast does not exist, and I am through discussing it. As for you." She turns to me. "I will decide your fate tomorrow."

Casper clenches his jaw. "Megan is with me, and she will stay with me. If you force her to leave, then I go with her. She is a part of us. She will help us win this war. As for you, you can stop lying to everyone and tell us the truth. Why have we been fighting over this Nuummite Jewel?"

She presses her lips in a tight line. "You are out of line, Casper. Do not challenge me." With that, she storms out of the room.

I haven't been in Belle Palais long and already I've caused a rift between Casper and his mom. I've caused a lot of tension and hatred within the palace and everywhere I go.

"Is there only one dragon?" Saida asks. "Where have you seen it?"

"When I first returned to Arvada. In the battlefield. He turned into the dragon. I-I stole the Jewel, then I had visions of Vincent and his father. Of the dragon. Of him throwing Casper off a cliff."

Saida's face twists in horror. "He threw you off a cliff?"

Casper nods. "Yes. Vincent has done many things to hurt us." I can't help but think that's directed at me.

"Because of you, isn't it? All of this is because of you?"

"Hey, lay off, Saida," Casper says. "She hasn't done anything."

"Yeah, except put your life in danger."

"All of this is because the Sprites want you all dead," I tell her, trying not to feel offended. "This war started long before we even met. Vincent's father,

King Jacques is determined to make Elves extinct. Somehow, the Elves believe they must have the Jewel, but they don't. I tried taking it away from Vincent, but it possessed me somehow into returning it."

Saida gives a sarcastic laugh. "Because you're a Sprite. You are toying with us. How can you trust her, Casper? It's obvious she's lying."

He sighs. "Saida, I have known her for years. The things she's done for me." He shakes his head. "She's on our side."

Cyran approaches us. "Tomorrow, let's discuss what to do."

Saida rolls her eyes. "Zev, did you see a dragon or are you entranced by her beauty like Casper is?"

Zev smirks. "Always so jealous. Yeah, I saw it. It was long ago. I never said anything because I thought it was my mind playing tricks."

"What about the Jewel?" Saida asks me. "Don't you think the reason you had to return it is because you're a Sprite and you're on their side?"

Tears cloud my vision. "I want to end the war."

"You could've been toying with Casper this whole time."

"Let's go. We'll finish this tomorrow." Silvyr places an arm on Saida's shoulder, urging her out of the room.

"I'm sorry for tonight." Cyran frowns. "I had hoped the Elves would be more welcoming. Perhaps with time. Please, try to feel at home and get some rest."

"Thanks," I tell him. Casper's friends are the only ones who seem to like me. Everyone else seems to be deathly afraid of me or like I'm going to surprise them with some kind of attack. Can't they see how much I love Casper and that I would do anything for him?

Casper takes my hand, and we worm our way through a maze of hallways and stairs until we reach his room.

Sitting on the edge of the bed, I take a deep breath. I can't help the exhaustion that rushes over me. The tears that fall down my cheeks. The guilt that knots in my stomach.

Casper moves in front of me, taking my hands in his. "I'm so sorry for that."

"You have nothing to be sorry for. I shouldn't be here."

"What?"

I shake my head.

"Talk to me, Megan. We've never kept anything from each other, and we shouldn't start now."

"I shouldn't be here. I've caused so many problems."

"Is this about going back to the human world?"

"I'm not a traitor, and it's clear I don't belong in this world. The Sprites want me dead, and the Elves think I'm an intruder. I feel lonely and if it weren't for you, I'd be seeking the witch for her help.

"I told you already that something hasn't felt right since I came back. I don't know why. Maybe I wasn't supposed to return here straight from a human form. It feels real but something is off. Almost like I'm not here. It's probably because no one has ever left a human world and entered an immortal world as they were dying. I don't think I was supposed to come here when I did or it could be that I've not been here in years and everything is so different, everyone is different. I don't even know how to be a Sprite anymore.

"I wish Vincent had never found us. I wish we were still living in the human world. Dancing at prom. Or swimming in the ocean. Climbing mountains to see beautiful nature. Playing dumb video games or watching movies. Being carefree. In love without a war brewing around us."

I take a deep breath. It will be okay. Everything is fine, I remind myself.

"Megan, war has not separated us. The fact that we are different species has not stopped me and certainly my mother will not stop me from being with you."

I take a deep breath. "They don't want me here, Casper. No one does. I feel so out of place I'm so afraid you'll see just how out of place I am. You'll realize you don't want me."

Casper pulls me to my feet and gathers me in his arms. Breathing in his scent calms me. He kisses the top of my head. He lifts my chin, forcing me to meet his eyes. "I know it's hard being here. No matter what happens, you and I are together. I always want you. After everything we've been through, it's still not enough to keep me away from you."

"I miss some of those things too, but this is where we live. This is our home."

"I know."

"Once we end the war, everything will be okay. Please don't go." I hear the panic in his voice.

"What is it?"

He exhales and I feel his air travel through my hair. "I don't want to lose you, Megan. I've lost you too many times."

"You won't. Why are you saying that?"

"I can't return to the human world."

"What? Why?"

"The witch forbids me to return. She said if I do, I will die."

"How? Is it because we came back here in our immortal form?"

"She said because of my Elf blood, once I come back to my immortal life, if I become mortal, I will age and die."

My heart falls. I had no idea that could happen. I never knew we would ever become humans. I'm not sure why I'm missing that life so much. If Casper can't return, it's not even an option. I won't leave him.

"I know it isn't easy right now but please stay with me. It will get better. You and I can make it a better place for everyone."

"I know."

"Your mother is hiding something. Everything we know is a lie. What have we been fighting for? A bunch of lies?"

He exhales. "Feels that way." It feels like his mother betrayed him and there is nothing I can say. "We've never been a lie," he says, looking at me.

"No. We aren't. I always thought of you. Even though Vincent told me you never loved me. I tried so hard not to give up hope. You gave me strength in one of the darkest times of my life. You were the light inside my darkness. You've always been that for me.

I kept thinking, if I survive this, I will search to the ends of the world for you and I will end the war."

"We will. I don't care how long it takes to convince them that our love is real."

Tears escape my eyes. I'm such a mess. Solitude will do that.

With his hands on either side of my face, he leans down, pressing his warm lips against mine. He slips his tongue past, grazing mine. Heat ignites throughout my body. Casper moves his mouth to my neck, and I melt into him. Teasing the straps of my dress, he moves me to the bed.

I love being in his arms, feeling safe and loved. He is everything to me and I would die for him. There are so many things we need to do right now; I want to enjoy what I can. I know Vincent will bring his army here. I know the dragon will appear. No matter what we're about to face, we have each other and these little moments together.

He crushes his lips against mine as he cradles my face with his hands. I lean back onto the bed and his hands slowly explore my body. My blood begins to boil as this intense heat moves throughout me.

He slowly pulls down my shirt, and he kisses my neck. It's as if he can't wait to get his hands on me but he takes his time. Slowly, he unbuttons my shirt, one button at a time. As he opens my shirt further, he lands kisses on my skin. It's almost too much sensation and I want more.

"I'll never leave you, Casper. I love you."

He kisses my forehead. "I love you. Are you happy?"

"Of course, I am. It doesn't matter where we are. As long as I'm with you. That's all that matters."

Casper crushes his lips to mine. "I want to you to be happy."

"I am."

I run my hands through his hair, and he returns his lips to mine. Each time he kisses me, my heart ignites with a new fire. I never want to extinguish it. My heart belongs to Casper. It always has and always will.

Twenty-Three

omething crashes, jolting me from my sleep. It's a bomb. The war found us. Voices shout and when my vision sharpens and I finally get my bearings, there's a man in a blue uniform pointing a gun at me.

I draw in a shaky breath.

Casper darts upright. "What are you doing?" Two other men pull him out of bed and slam him against the wall, placing him in shackles.

The Sprites found us, but the uniforms are wrong. This has to be a dream.

A man with short red hair throws a dress at me. "Get dressed."

They give me the decency to slip on the dress, then he takes my wrist, snapping shackles around them. "You are being summoned by the Queen," he says.

"You can't do this," Casper demands and struggles with the two officers. "Let her go. She didn't do anything."

One of the guards slams the butt of his rifle against Casper's stomach. He doubles over but the guard brings him upright.

"Wanna tell me what I can or can't do again?"

"Megan didn't do anything."

"She's the enemy who has trespassed."

"What? No."

Casper elbows the guard in the face, breaking free.

The redheaded guard aims his gun at Casper's head. "Move one more inch and I will have no choice but to shoot."

"Casper, don't," I tell him.

The blonde guard holds his face and moans. He restrains Casper and slams the butt of his gun into his face again, knocking him out.

"No!" I shout.

"Dammit, she said not to injure them," the redheaded man says. "Come on."

They escort Casper and me from the room.

My heart thrashes against my ribcage as nerves wrap around my stomach like a vice grip. Will the Queen believe me? Will she be convinced enough of our love? I have to try.

"Please, you don't have to do this," I tell the officers.

The one who has a tight hold on my arm jerks me. "You're a piece of filth that belongs at the bottom of the ocean."

I swallow hard. What are they going to do to me? How did the Queen find out I was here? Was it Saida? Maybe it was Vaelyn. Maybe she ran to the Queen after we met with her. It could've been anyone. I feel sick. I need to break free, but I can't leave Casper. They take us outside where it's humid but cool. Lightning bugs twinkle greenish-yellow lights all around us. It's strange walking through such a beautiful place yet scared out of my mind.

We make the long walk to another castle. It's hidden behind thick woods and there are more Elves staring and watching. I hear their disgusted noises and words. Walking inside, the castle looks identical to the other one but bigger.

It would be impressive if officers weren't dragging me inside against my will in the middle of the night. I have not done anything, but it doesn't matter. I shouldn't have come. Casper and I should've gone to the witch and escaped. No one wants us here. We cannot win this war if both sides are against us.

The Queen sits in a tall-backed chair with an unamused look on her face. She's gorgeous with long black hair that reaches her hips, her amber eyes are surrounded by dark eye makeup. Her intense stare could kill. Her crown is collection of silver branches with antique bronze outlining.

"So, you're the Sprite who has everyone gasping in horror," she says.

"I'm Megan." Blood rushes to my cheeks.

"I'm Ena, Queen of the Elves. I am quite curious as to why you are here."

Casper groans and when he wakes, he starts to struggle. When he sees Ena, he stops.

I swallow hard. "Casper saved me from the Sprites and brought me here to safety."

She cocks an eyebrow. "Safety from your own kind. That means you are a traitor."

"No, Your Majesty. I am in love with Casper, and they want me dead because of it."

"In love with your enemy? Sounds traitorous to me. Either way, I highly doubt that you are in love with him."

"She is," Casper says. "And I am in love with her."

Ena smiles, but her eyes are cold. "You have been bewitched, my dear."

"No. I love him, and I want to be with him. If I could stay here—"

She laughs. "You're joking? Why should I protect you? Are you of any importance? You ran away from your own kind. I can only imagine why they'd want you dead. Those who betray must pay for their crimes." Her glance moves to Casper. "This is why you went out of your way to rescue her? Please tell me there is more to this *Sprite*."

Clenching my teeth, I take a deep breath, wishing they would release me from the shackles. "Whether you believe me or not, you need to know that the Nuummite Jewel isn't to keep the Elves alive," I begin, and she raises an eyebrow. "It's to keep Vincent from becoming a dragon."

"You know where the Jewel is?"

"Yes. Vincent has it."

Ena looks at me like I've completely lost my mind. "Am I supposed to know who Vincent is?"

"He's a Sprite. And an Elf. His father is conspiring to kill all of the Elves by using Vincent as a weapon."

"Please, you must listen to me. I know it sounds crazy but it's the truth."

"First of all, dragons no longer exist. Second, there has never been a mixing of our breeds, nor will there ever be. That alone is laughable. For you to speak such ridiculousness." She shakes her head. "I hear you proposed to this creature."

"It's true," Casper says. "I've seen the dragon."

I know he hasn't and he's just telling her that.

She narrows her eyes. "I highly doubt that."

Silvyr approaches. "Your Majesty if I may speak. The dragon exists."

"These are incredulous claims. There have been no sightings of dragons in centuries. The punishment for lying to your Queen is rather severe."

"Please you have to believe me."

"Why? How do I know you're not here as a spy for those wretched Sprites?"

"Why would you think that?"

"You're a Sprite. You're all liars. How do I know Sprites aren't about to attack us because you led them right to us? It is no surprise how she has you wrapped around her little finger," she tells Casper.

"You don't know what you're talking about," he says.

Ena stands, tall and strong. It makes her even more intimidating. Her long dark robes drag across the floor as she moves. "No? I know their magic. I know the spells they put on others to manipulate and control."

"I know that too, more than anything," I tell her. "I've experienced it from Vincent numerous times. Even if I had that power, I would never do that to Casper or anyone."

She scoffs with a smile.

"You don't know the hell she's been through," Casper says. "You don't know what she's done for me. She's on our side."

"Is she? Or is she plotting against you and all of us? Do we need to prepare for the Sprites to attack us? Your bringing her here has put us in danger. Sprites are elaborate with their tricks. They last months or even decades sometimes."

"We need to attack the Sprites. Especially King Jacques. He's controlling Vincent and will unleash the dragon."

"Sounds like a scheming plot to me. We go after the Sprites and suddenly we are ambushed. Taken for hostages and tortured. I do not know who Vincent is, nor do I care. You've wasted your time and mine for coming here. My army will do fine without you."

I grit my teeth, knowing I should keep my mouth shut. "Your army doesn't even know what they're fighting for. The Elves have been fighting this war for decades thinking they're fighting to save a Jewel that has no relevance to them at all. You aren't going to tell them the truth. You call me a liar, but you and every leader of the Elves have been lying to your people all this time. You're a leader. Why are you hiding the truth? Why are you so afraid to tell them the truth?"

"How dare you speak to me in such a way. Get her out of my chambers."

The officer grabs me again.

"Are you okay with your people dying at your hands over a lie? Why aren't you protecting them? What's in it for you to keep this war going?"

She moves right in front of me, and I see something flash in her eyes. Fear? "You have no idea what you speak of."

I swallow hard, knowing I've hit a nerve. "You know I'm right."

"You want the Jewel? I can kill Vincent to get it," Casper says.

My eyes snap to his. Why did he say that? He can't kill Vincent alone. Vincent's tried killing him too many times.

Ena lets out a hearty laugh along with a few officers. "You? Kill a dragon? How do you suppose you do that?"

"He's tried killing me. I'm ready. I'm the only one who can do this."

"You both must take me for a fool to believe all these allegations."

"The dragon is real," someone behind us says. "There are multiple ones."

I twist around to see a girl with dark hair. "Multiple?"

"Yes."

Ena stops laughing and shakes her head. "Enough of this nonsense. There are no dragons." Her voice is full of malice. "I do not want to hear another word of it. Take her to the cells."

The guards urge me toward the door.

Casper wrestles against the two men holding him. "No!"

Ena faces Casper. "You will receive punishment for bringing this disgusting creature here."

I'm so angry that I want to cry. It will take a lot to convince Ena, and I have to do whatever it will take. I could lure the dragon here. Somehow. Without endangering anyone's life.

I have to do something.

"Wait, please!" I cry, turning around. "I will do anything to prove to you that I am on your side," I tell her, almost regretting it.

She tilts her head and holds up her hands at the guards and they stop. Now I have her attention. "Anything?"

"Yes." I'm breathing hard, hoping that she changes her mind. Hoping that I can come up with something to prove it to her.

"We'll do whatever we can as long as we aren't separated or killed," Casper adds.

Ena holds up her hand to silence Casper. She approaches me, and as she talks, she circles me like a prey. "The Sprites have extraordinary magic and they have used it to torture the Elves long enough. I don't trust you at all. I also know you haven't used any magic on me or Casper that I can tell."

"I have no magic."

She studies me. "You do and it seems you were never taught to use it. I've never known a Sprite so naïve. I mean that as a compliment."

"How would you even know if I used magic?"

"I have my ways."

"I don't have any magic. No powers. I was born this way."

"Something happened to you to make you forget. Perhaps you're very good at hiding the truth. Maybe that is your power."

I shake my head. "I was born without powers." Her words make me think of Vincent. Could he have made me forget that about myself?

"I do not have time or patience to argue with you. Until you realize that you can be of any help to me, you will stay in the cellars. Take her."

The guards grab my arms and I exchange a look with Casper. "No! Please, you must believe me," I scream.

Casper moves toward me, but they catch him.

Staring at Casper urgently, I struggle with the Elves, breaking free. I rush up to him pressing my lips to his, hoping that by kissing him we'll magically be transported into another world together.

The guards pull me away. Away from the one person who keeps me sane. Why is everyone trying so hard to keep us apart? Why isn't love ever enough? What does it matter that we're different? How does our love affect so many people? I will never understand it. I will never understand how what I do in my life angers others, when I mean no harm.

I don't know what will happen. The Elves act like I'm the most dangerous person they've ever met. Just because of who I am, I'm automatically evil.

Maybe I am. Maybe I need to be locked up. I'm used to it. I'm used to the coldness. The loneliness.

Nothing will change. The Elves and Sprites will always hate each other. They will forever kill each other. This hatred will continue to bleed and I'm beginning to feel like there is nothing I can do. Both sides need to be educated, but both are too stubborn. They only know what they've been taught their entire lives. Maybe both leaders should be locked up or killed. Maybe the Jewel needs to be destroyed once and for all.

The guards throw me in the familiar cell. When they lock me in, I fall to my knees in a silent cry. No matter what, I will always be a prisoner to someone.

Twenty-Four

count the cracks in the floor. Sixty-eight.

The bars on my door. Twelve.

The seconds in my head. Three thousand fifty-two.

Anything so I don't go crazy. I don't know what Ena expects of me. Trying to prove myself to people is exhausting. I know hearing about dragons doesn't help but they have to believe me. They have to be prepared for what's to come. I shouldn't have attacked her like that though. It was a last resort.

When I hear shuffling, my heart skips a beat. Is it Casper?

"Megan." Ena greets me. She's wearing a beautiful navy gown with flared sleeves. Dark makeup surrounds her amber eyes. Her beauty doesn't fit in with the dinginess of the cell. "I've had a lot of time to think about your rather unfortunate situation. I've decided that you can be useful to me."

"How?" I ask, cringing when I hear how hoarse my voice is.

"First, you need to figure out your powers. Every Sprite has one and whoever told you otherwise lied to you."

"Why are you so insistent on this?"

"Because I can use you."

"Use me how? I've already offered to help bring down King Jacques, what more could you want?"

"Well, that depends on what your magic is. I don't trust you to take down the King. You've had numerous chances, yet they almost killed you and you would have died had it not been for Casper and a few other of my Elves. By you coming here, you've led them to us."

"I didn't lead them to you. They already know where you reside."

"No, they don't. They have never known because we have protected this land for centuries. Your being here changes that."

"Don't you think Casper used the proper channel to bring me here and not let anyone follow us?"

"I don't know. I can't trust him. He has gone against everything we stand for. And for what? Absolutely nothing."

I have never hated an Elf until I met Ena. She is impossible. Getting to my feet, I stand near the cell bars. "I am not nothing. If you ever felt an ounce of love, maybe you would know what that feels like. Do you store all that hatred inside you and lash out at anyone who says no to you? You can't hurt me. Do your worst. The Sprites have already done that. I've already been a prisoner most of my existence."

She smirks. "You are in no position to challenge me."

"This isn't the first time I've been locked up. I've escaped every single time."

"Good for you. Yet, you never killed a single Sprite during your escapes. You've never stopped the enemy you are supposedly against. You've done nothing."

That stings. She's right though. I have nothing to show for it. "I plan to change that." The words escape before I can stop them. It surprises me that I would say that.

Ena nods. "I'm sure. In the meantime, you should work on figuring out your magic or your time will run out."

"I don't even know where to begin."

"I put you in here to figure that out. Perhaps, I can give you an incentive." She gestures with her hand and two guards bring in a prisoner. He's bound by metal shackles and dirt covers his face and body. As he appears closer, I gasp. Casper's face is bloodied and cut in several places. When his eyes meet mine, I crumble.

I squeeze the metal bars of my cell, wanting to get closer to him. Wanting to touch him. "What have you done to him?"

"Megan," he tries to say, and the guard punches him.

"Stop!" I yell, knowing I can't stop them.

"If you care for this man, you will find your magic. If you can't find it, I'll know you are just another disgusting, selfish Sprite."

"Why are you doing this?"

She approaches my cell with a daring smile. "This man has risked his life multiple times to save you. I need to be sure you've been worth it. For once, you should risk your life to save his. Shouldn't be too difficult since you love him so much."

I clench my teeth, willing the tears away. "Fine. I will do what you want. Once I figure out my magic, then what?"

"You want to be part of us, you'll use your magic to kill all of these Sprite prisoners." She points to the cells surrounding mine. "Then you will bring me the Jewel."

"You're a monster. I can't kill the Sprites. King Jacques has brainwashed them. Like you have with the Elves."

"I thought you said you would do anything. Anything for Casper."

I shake my head. "We don't have to perform genocide. Not all of them deserve to die. Same with the Elves. This war will only continue if both sides feel that way. All we have to do is imprison King Jacques."

Ena scoffs. "Such a sad, naïve little girl. You know we can't just arrest the leader, and everything be right in the world."

"Why do you want the Jewel so much? It holds no value."

"It does to me, as well as the Elves."

"I can't do this."

"If you can't prove your loyalty to me, then you will remain in this cell. Forever. Once proven, you can be useful in leading my army right to the source, so we can kill them all. I will have the Jewel. Your freedom will be granted."

"You are just like the Sprites. Why do you want innocent people to die?"

"Innocent?" she spits. "These people are not innocent, I assure you. Take this woman for example." She waves her hand, and a guard opens a cell. They heave a woman out. Her mass of blonde hair is knotted and dirty. The woman is emaciated and wears no shoes. Ena forces her to look up and I gasp.

Florence.

Staring at my best friend shakes me to my core. All this time I thought she had died. She's been a prisoner of the Elves for who knows how long. My heart crumbles as I stare at her tired and worn face.

"By the look of your face, I'd say you know this woman," Ena says.

I turn to her. "Why is she a prisoner? She ran away with Edmond, one of your own. She loved him."

Ena chuckles. "She sold you out. Along with our beloved Edmond. She was caught by Sprites and sent Edmond with them. She also told your other Sprites where you and Casper ran away to. That's how they found you. Haven't you ever wondered how the Sprites always found you? Sounds like you should figure out who you can trust. And you cannot trust Sprites."

Ena jerks Florence back into her cell and turns to me. "It's your choice, Megan."

"What? You can't possibly expect me to figure this out. I don't even know what to look for or how to find it or even where to look."

"You will figure it out unless your love for Casper isn't real. There is one more thing. This…Vincent fellow. Why did he try to kill Casper so many times?"

"Because I'm in love with Casper."

"There's more to him, isn't there?" She studies me. "Otherwise, you would have killed him already."

Confused, I meet her eyes, wondering why she's curious. "I don't kill."

"Ah, a martyr. He must mean something to you then. Are you in love with him and playing Casper for a fool?"

At this, Casper raises his head.

"What? No. Vincent is nothing to me. He tortured and manipulated me for years."

Ena crosses her arms in front of her chest. "You two were very close at one point in time. I see it."

"You don't see anything. Yes, I was in love with him at a point in my life, what does that matter?"

"It matters because if this man is as dangerous as you say he is, you let him off the hook time and time again. I want to know why."

"I fell in love with him when I didn't know who he truly was."

"Ahh. Now you want Casper to do your dirty work because you no longer love Vincent?" She studies me as if she can see right through me. "All I see are happy memories of you and Vincent."

A blush creeps up my cheeks. Can she see inside my mind? If she could, she could see the horrible things Vincent has done to me. "You need to pay more attention."

Ena cocks that right eyebrow and gives a sly smile. "You seem to be more in love with Vincent."

"You couldn't be more wrong."

"Bring the Jewel to me." She signals the guards, and they take Casper and my heart with him.

What is Ena trying to prove? Why does she suddenly want to know about Vincent? Is she hiding something? Is she trying to cause a rift between Casper and me? He can't believe what she says.

Now to prove myself to the Elves, I must get the Jewel and kill every prisoner. Including Florence. How can she possibly think I would kill my best friend?

Because she knows I won't. She knew this all along. She isn't going to help me, knowing I possess no magic at all.

There is only one way I'll be able to possess the Jewel and that means killing Vincent. But no matter how much Vincent has done to me, I have never wished for his death. What would that say about me if I did? It won't solve anything. The hurt, the pain, the chaos inside my head will still be there.

We have to end the curse. I don't know how to get out of this. If I can't kill Vincent and the Sprites, I'll never be free.

Twenty-Five

Hugging my knees to my chest, I lean my head against the cold stone wall. I'm trembling from the cold and my stomach growls. Someone told the Queen I was here in Belle Palais. Maybe it would've gone differently had we not hidden, but I can't blame Casper for that.

Even as I think it, I know she doesn't believe me and doesn't care.

"Megan?" I hear her familiar voice from across the way.

"Florence?"

She presses her face against the cell bars and looks up with tears in her eyes. "Megan, I thought I'd never see you again."

My chin quivers. I haven't seen her in so long. In a way she kinda reminds me of Cherry. My heart aches a little from thinking about her.

"Vincent told me you died," I say.

"No. He found Edmond and me, then killed Edmond. Just...killed him. I never sold Edmond out. I would never do that. I love him. Ena's lying."

"How did the Elves capture you?"

"After they killed Edmond, they captured me, threatening to take me back to the Sprites to be hanged, but I escaped from Vincent. I had to. I ran right to the Elves, thinking they would welcome me since one of their own loved me. I never thought I would be taken as a prisoner. They don't trust any of us. I came here seeking refuge." Tears roll down her cheeks.

Hearing her story breaks my heart. I abandoned my friend. "I'm so sorry. Have you been in here the whole time Casper and I were gone?"

She nods.

"I'm so sorry."

"Edmond and I were happy. Even if it was for a short period of time. A love so great, so unimaginable and I got to experience it. Not a lot of people can say they have. At least I had that."

I feel awful. I ran away and lived so many lives with Casper, while my best friend has been locked up and only had happiness for a short time. I will make it up to her though.

"Please don't kill us. I never turned against you or Edmond. I never had him killed."

"I would never kill you, Florence. I promise I will find a way out of this. I will release you and the others.

You don't deserve to be chained up. I'm so sorry this happened."

"I've missed you so much."

"Me, too."

"I don't understand how or why you're here."

"It's a long story." I launch into the whole story starting with the second Casper and I found the witch and drank the potion. I tell her about the Jewel...dragons...King Jacques.

Florence gasps and sighs through most of it. "Wow. How did Vincent find you?"

I shake my head. "I don't know."

"Do you still love Vincent?"

"No. I still have hope for him that maybe he can see how much better he is than his father."

"You're a much better person than me. I wouldn't have hesitated in killing someone who tortured me."

"It isn't his fault. His father has controlled him his entire life."

"Still, Vincent isn't a good person. Why do you want to save him?"

"I...I couldn't have fallen in love with such a monster. There has to be some good left inside of him. He can't be all evil, can he?"

Florence shrugs and frowns.

"I am a terrible friend. Vincent said you died. I should've come looking for you. I should've—"

"Megan, it's okay. You had to find your happiness and you did. You're together."

"Not anymore. You saw what Ena did to Casper. He's a prisoner, too."

"You're both alive and you're both here."

"I know. This is no way to live though."

Florence nods. "I know. What if you both went back to the human world?"

"We can't. At least, Casper can't return. The witch told him he would die if he did."

"What? How can the Elves do this to Casper? He's one of their own kind."

"Anyone who betrays the Queen, or their own kind has to be punished," a voice from one of the cells speaks. He sounds ragged and exhausted.

"How long have you been locked up?" I ask.

"I don't even know."

"What did you do?"

He's silent for several minutes. "I killed an Elf. A Sprite got into my head."

Tears collect at the base of my throat. Sprites haven't been the best and the more I hear how awful we've been, the more I feel the urge to end this war.

"Why would they keep you here so long only to kill you? That doesn't make any sense."

"Torture," the man says. "A fate worse than death."

"Exactly," Florence says. "You should know that."

I nod. "What's your name?" I ask the man.

"Nyx."

"I'm sorry this happened to you."

"You must figure out your power," Florence says.

"I don't even know how. She thinks I have some, but I've never had any kind of magic."

"I can help you."

"How?"

Florence lets out a breath. "Megan, the Queen is right. You have one. Vincent always made you forget it."

My heart drops. "What?"

"I'm sorry. I never told you because he made me forget, too. Being in here for so long has made his charm or whatever wear off. I remember so much now."

Sitting beside the bars, I rest my head against the cold iron. Vincent. He covered his tracks for everything. Until I stole his necklace. If Vincent made me forget about Casper and my life with him and it always came back to me, surely the memories and knowledge of me possessing a power would, too. But they haven't. Ever.

"You don't happen to know what that magic is, do you?"

"I don't," she says. "Think about your strongest traits. You're honest and you hide nothing."

I don't know where to begin with those, but I have to concentrate. I must save Casper. I refuse to live in a world without him.

Twenty-Six

eat washes over me and my stomach churns. Every time I move my head, the cell bars sway and swirl. I don't know how many days it's been. I don't even know if Casper is okay. The Queen hasn't been down here in a while and part of me wonders if the Sprites didn't already attack and left us in this underground cell.

Every day I've tried to figure out what my power could be, and every day I fail. My heart sinks each time. I know if I don't find out soon, she will kill Casper or keep torturing him. He did nothing wrong, and I hate how everyone tries to keep us apart.

Bits and pieces of memories of us together in our human life flash in my mind. Like the time we cuddled in bed and talked all night after the party where

Adam attacked me. When he took me to the beach for a week and it was beautiful. We were happy. Carefree. The memories only make me wish for our human life and that strong feeling overcomes me. The feeling of a cruel wanting for something I know I can never have. I don't even know why I long for that world so much, but deep down I know. It's miserable in Arvada. Everyone is warring. No one trusts anyone and we are all being tested.

I have a hard time keeping my head up. My lips are painfully dry and the more I lick and bite them, the more they bleed and crack. As I stare at the concrete floor, I imagine food and water. A whole turkey. Potatoes. Vegetables. Soups. Desserts. My mouth salivates. The food disappears and I close my eyes.

"Did...did you just do that?" Florence asks.

"Do what?"

"Make the food appear? I saw it and then it was gone."

"You saw that? I...I just imagined it."

Florence gasps. "Megan! That's your power. Show me something else."

My hear skips a beat. Have I figured it out? "Like what?"

"Anything."

This is crazy. How can she see my imagination? Can she read my mind? "Did anyone else see it?"

"I did," Nyx says. "I saw the turkey and the desserts."

"I saw it too," Fara, the girl across the way next to Florence says.

"You can make us see things," Florence says. "You can make anyone see anything."

I'm not sure how to react. I don't know what I should do with this power if anything.

"What else can you make us see?" Fara asks. She approaches the bars of her cells. Her brown hair is matted, and I see the gold specks in her brown eyes. How many Elves are locked up in here?

"I-I don't know." I stare at her and imagine what she looked like before being captivity. Long shimmering brown hair. Fresh milky skin with little freckles across her nose.

"Wow," Florence says. "She's beautiful."

The girl looks down and stares at her hair. "My hair. It-it's soft." When she meets my eyes, tears fall down her cheeks.

"Maybe you can make us all appear dead," Nyx says.

"What?" I ask. "Why would I do that?"

"Maybe we can use it to our advantage. Try it."

I inhale and stare at Fara across the way. Her body slumps against the bars as her arm hangs out, blood pooling around.

"Wow. That is crazy," Florence says.

"Will Queen Ena believe it?"

"She may. Only one way to find out."

For the first time in a long time, I feel hopeful. I try not to cling to it too tightly.

Every night, a guard comes by each of our cells and ladles out some type of soup in our dingy metal bowl. I never know what's in the soup and I'm in no position to be choosy about my food. At least we're being fed. If we don't place our bowls in the corner of our cells, we don't get fed. If they call out to us without an answer, they check on us to see if we're still alive.

The guard, who looks no older than a twenty-year-old with short blond hair, quickly scoops the soup into our bowls, sloshing some of it out onto the floor. When he reaches Nyx's cell, he gives him his food, but Nyx doesn't move.

"Hey, boy. It's dinnertime," he says.

Nothing.

He lets out a frustrated sigh. "We have a dead one, Flynn" he calls and when another guard approaches, he unlocks Nyx's cell. He nudges Nyx with his foot and Nyx rolls over. No movement. No breath. Nyx isn't dead but I want to see how much they believe the illusion. I wonder if we can pretend to be dead and escape the prison. Shaking my head, I know that won't be possible. There are too many guards. I don't think I'm that strong.

"What did you do, Joffrey?" Flynn asks. "Did you kill him?"

Joffrey sighs. "No. He died."

"How?"

"How should I know? It's probably this sorry excuse for food."

"What a waste. They don't even deserve food. We should've killed them on sight."

I hate how the guards show no remorse or talk about us like we aren't living, breathing beings. It's like we are taking up space to them, which I guess technically we are.

Joffrey shrugs. "The Queen seems to think they're valuable assets."

Flynn scoffs. "Valuable. The only thing they're good for is a punching bag."

I grit my teeth, trying to ignore their words. *Focus on the illusion.*

Nyx starts laughing. Both Joffrey and Flynn jump back. Flynn punches Nyx in the face and kicks him in the stomach. He hits him again.

"Hey!" I call out and both guards look up. "Leave him alone."

"This doesn't concern you, filth."

"Why don't you tell the Queen I'm ready to see her?"

Joffrey makes his way to my cell. "Why don't you pipe down?"

Getting to my feet, I stare at Joffrey. I can see fear in his pale green eyes even though he's trying hard to hide it. He's afraid of me, which is strange because I can't hurt him. Doesn't he know that? He's seen me in here for days or weeks without hurting him. Or is it the simple fact that I'm a Sprite? Doesn't care who I am, only that I'm an enemy. That's how they were taught. Taught to hate something they don't understand.

"Tell the Queen I'm ready for her."

He studies me with caution. "Like you have any powers. You know Casper is better than you and the Queen is proving that. She's already gotten him back to the right state of mind. He doesn't want you. He never wanted you."

"If that's true, maybe he should be the one to tell me, instead of some messenger boy," I tell him, keeping my voice strong, even though I'm seconds from falling apart. I know he's only trying to get a rise out of me, and I can't let him know that it's slowly working.

A muscle in Joffrey's jaw twitches. "You're playing Casper. The Queen sees right through you. You're a traitor and you will die down here like so many before you." I don't miss the hint of hesitation in his voice. I have to use this to my advantage.

Curling my fingers around the cell bars, I inch closer, pinning him with my stare. "You have no idea who I am or what I can do." I give him the illusion of changing my appearance, and he gasps. To him, I look exactly like the Queen.

He swallows hard and averts his eyes for a second. "Eat your food."

I let out a short laugh, still appearing as the Queen. "What's wrong, Joffrey? Afraid of a little magic?"

Flynn crosses over toward us and bangs his hand on the cell bars. "Shut up, you crazy witch. Come on," he tells Joffrey.

Once they leave the room, I release a breath. My hands shake as adrenaline shoots through my veins. The pounding in my chest reaches my ears and I smile. I'd never done anything like that before and I loved it.

"Brilliant," I hear Nyx say.

"I don't know what I'm doing." My voice trembles and I have to control it so Ena can't see my fear. I have to learn to put on a brave face.

"Joffrey is scared of you," Fara says.

"I don't know why."

"After that stunt, who wouldn't be?" Florence says.

"You're new," Nyx chimes in. "And you're involved with one of his kind."

"I'm sorry they beat you," I tell him.

"Don't be. They can beat me all they want. They still won't ever defeat me."

Being locked up for several years hasn't deterred Nyx and I admire him for that. I've been a prisoner most of my life it seems and there have been moments when I was ready to give up. I've always kept going though.

This new resounding excitement dashes through my veins. I never knew I had any kind of power like this inside of me. Is that why Vincent made me forget? Did he think I would use it against him? Knowing that I can appear as anyone or make others see things that aren't there, ideas churn in my head with how to defeat King Jacques.

Twenty-Seven

small crack of light seeps through the ceiling at the end of the dungeon. As I stare at the light, I try to remember how warm the sun is. How it made me feel. I long to see the sunlight. I don't even know if it's morning, noon, or dusk. I remember the days when Casper and I lounged in the warm sun at his pool. We spent a lot of time there. Memories of our human lives are mixing together like a pot of soup. I keep picturing us in our most recent human life, but the actual memories are from another lifetime.

Rolling onto my back, I wince. Sleeping on the stone floor hurts my back, yet somehow, I've gotten used to it. My right side is numb from staying in the same position for many hours. I get to my feet so I can stretch. I'm so tired of these same three walls. I miss Casper. I have no idea where he is or if he's okay. Part of me thinks that maybe I should give up on us. I have no idea how we can ever truly be happy when someone tries to kill us or kidnap us or hold us hostage.

I hear motion toward the door and my body becomes rigid. Several guards line the entrance, guns ready. My heart hammers inside my chest as I press my back against a wall. The Queen enters, dressed in an elegant golden dress. Her black hair snakes its way on one side of her neck to her stomach in large bouncy curls.

"The guards tell me you've figured out your power," Ena says, stopping in front of my cell.

"I have." With my mind, I give her an image of all the prisoners dead. Florence's body rests against the bars as blood seeps out. Fara's face is pressed against her gate, a dead look in her eyes.

I unlock my cell.

She scans the room, then back at me. "Mind tricks, I see. Could be useful."

I don't stop the imagination and transform myself to look like her. I know she sees me walk out of the cell and move toward her. She stares at me; her eyes widen with each step. I reach for her arm and when I touch it, she jumps back.

I stop the hallucination. "I can make anyone see what I want. I can make them feel what I want."

A smile spreads across Ena's face. "You will be instrumental in my army."

I return the smile. "Only if you release Casper."

She purses her lips together and begins to pace. Her long skirt drags across the concrete floor. "Casper is in a good place."

"Didn't seem like it the other day."

"Oh that." She waves her hand dismissively. "That was for show, and it worked. I need you to do something else for me to prove your allegiance. Once you do that, I will grant your freedom."

"What more do you want? You already want me to kill Sprites and Vincent and somehow bring the Jewel to you, which is going to be impossible. Vincent wears it constantly. Once he sees me, he'll lock me up. That's why I need the Elves' help."

She moves closer to my cell. "You showed me you can be whomever you want. I'm fairly certain you can trick him."

"I can't take the Jewel from him. I tried that already, and it possessed me to bring it back to Vincent."

"Because you are weak. You still love him and that is why you will never overpower him."

I can feel my temper rising. "You're joking, right? Why do you keep saying that? I want nothing to do with him."

"Yet, you are still hopeful he can change. I know he won't kill you. If he wanted you dead, he would've done that already. Negotiate with him. Trick him. Do whatever you have to do."

"It isn't that simple."

"Sure, it is. If he brings an army, so be it. We will be ready."

"Do I get any kind of protection?"

"You don't need any."

"Okay, fine. After you get the Jewel, then what else do you want? Your list is growing. I'm in love with an Elf. How does that not already prove my allegiance to you?"

"That proves nothing. You can very well fake being in love. I've seen it happen before."

"What is it you want me to do?"

"You need to forget about Casper. If you want your freedom, you need to let him go."

Her words take me off guard. "What?"

"I am working with him to return him to who he's supposed to be. You two cannot be together."

"Who are you to keep us apart?"

She cocks that eyebrow again. "I am the Queen of Elves, and it is forbidden for a Sprite and Elf to be together. You know this. When I'm through with Casper, he will want nothing to do with you. I'm telling you; you must forget about him in order to gain your freedom. Otherwise, you will remain a prisoner forever."

"Why?" I try so hard to hide my quivering chin.

"You are not meant to be together. Think about it. How hard has it been for you two to be together? The powers that be are trying to tell you something."

"Whatever. You can't keep us apart. What if you release me, and I run away?"

The corners of her mouth lift like she knows my bluff. "Where will you go? No one wants you. I know you won't run away, because you love both Casper and Vincent and you would never leave them both behind. If you do, you will be killed. Either by one of us or one of them. The choice is yours, Megan." Ena turns her back and leaves the room with all of the guards.

The room is silent except for the pounding in my chest. Sliding down to the ground, I give in to the tears. If only for a moment. Vincent was right. The Elves will never accept me as one of their own. Why did I ever think they would? How am I supposed to forget Casper? The thought twists inside me like a knife. How am I supposed to steal the Jewel again? I'm not strong enough.

But I have to be. For Casper. Unless she won't kill him. I can't take that chance. Even if I can never see him again, knowing he's alive will be enough for me.

"You have to do this," Florence says.

"What?" I look up, letting tears fall down my cheeks. "How am I supposed to forget Casper? How am I supposed to go back to Vincent without any protection? I can't steal the Jewel again. I can't kill him."

"You have to try. To save Casper."

I rub my tired face. I have to confront the person who has made my life miserable in order to save the man I love, yet I'm not allowed to ever see him again.

"Use your powers," Fara says. "Pretend you died in your cell. Then go find Casper."

"They'll check my pulse and know I'm lying."

"They didn't even check Nyx when you placed an illusion over him."

"Now that they know my power, they'll expect me to use it. They'll check it."

"Megan, you can't give up," Florence says. "She is going to kill Casper. You have to try."

"I know. I'm not strong enough to kill Vincent."

"You have to be. You have to end this war."

Feeling the weight of the world on my shoulders, I draw my knees to my chest. Maybe I can use my power to trick Vincent. By some miracle, I can return the Jewel to Queen Ena. Then maybe I can pretend to be an Elf so that I can be with Casper.

I refuse to let him go. I refuse to believe she's controlling him to forget about me. He would never let anyone do that to him. If he doesn't have a choice, I can only imagine what she's done to him.

Maybe I can trick the witch into changing his appearance so we can escape back to the human world. This can't be the end of Casper and me. We didn't get enough time. Though, no amount of time is ever enough with him.

All throughout the night, Ena's words repeat in my head along with ideas of escaping all of it. I've made my decision. I will accept her offer and hope that Vincent can't see right through me.

When Queen Ena returns with her entourage, she crosses her arms as she awaits my answer.

"I will do it," I tell her. "On one condition."

She raises an eyebrow and smirks. "Go ahead."

"If you are forbidding Casper and me to ever see each other again, you must let me see him one more time before I leave."

Ena mulls it over and finally she nods. "Okay. I will arrange for you to see him tonight. Then, tomorrow you will leave."

My pulse edges higher with the promise of seeing Casper. I will tell him my plan and I'll see how far gone he is, according to Queen Ena. Where are they keeping him? If he's a prisoner or traitor, why isn't he down here with the rest of us?

"Fine," I say.

The rest of the night, I bide my time. It slowly inches forward, almost like sitting at a green light that's about to turn yellow and I have to wait for that last car to clear the intersection, but they seem to move in slow motion.

The hours drag on. I don't know what day it is. I lay down and try to sleep. Sleep always passes the time. I long to dream of Casper. I long for the time in our lives when we will be free. Tired of being locked up, held against my will, no matter what I do. No matter how I act or what I say. I am never free.

I have to get out of here. I can't live like this much longer.

Twenty-Eight

wake with a start. Sitting up, I hear faint screeching sounds. Straining to hear, I know it can't be what I think it is. My heart knocks wildly in my chest. Something explodes above and the cells tremble causing small bits of the wall to crumble in the cell. I get to my feet.

"What was that?" Florence asks.

"Dragons." I know it is. It has to be. Nothing else makes that sound.

"What?" Fara stands, fear in her eyes. "They really do exist?"

Voices amplify as they enter the dungeon. Queen Ena storms into the room charging toward my cell in a flowy, gold gown. "What do you think you're doing? How dare you?"

"What?"

"Open her door," she demands Joffrey. He does and she seizes my throat, pulling me toward her.

She slams me against the wall. "Make the illusion stop."

"What? What are you talking about?" I choke through my words. Her fingers tighten around my neck slightly cutting off my air.

"Don't play stupid! You are causing panic across the castle. Stop the illusion of the dragons."

Dragons. The high-pitched sound is exactly what I thought it was. "Vincent."

Ena slams me into the wall again. "Stop this nonsense. You are not helping your cause by making everyone see dragons. They do not exist."

"This isn't me. This is happening." I claw at her hands to release me.

I see the slight panic in her eyes, then she regains her confidence. "End this now, or I will have Joffrey shoot you."

As on cue, Joffrey raises his weapon to my temple. "Just give me the word."

"No, please. I'm not doing this."

Ena nods to Joffrey. He cocks the gun. The ground shakes and Ena loses her grip on me. Joffrey lowers his gun. Rocks and dust fall over us as thunderous sounds rumble above.

"I promise you. I am not doing this."

"The Sprites are attacking."

"We have to get out of here."

Ena shakes her head. "You must turn yourself in to the Sprites. They want you. In order to get them to stop, you must give yourself up."

"No, please," I beg. "Give me a chance to prove it to you. We can defeat them."

"Your Majesty, we need to go," Joffrey says.

The ceiling caves in sending the three of us to the ground. I cover my head as the stone walls crumble creating dust clouds but it's no use. Rocks hit my head hard enough to send the world spinning. I feel cold air blasting through the dungeon as the strong wind kicks up more of the dust. A loud ringing sounds in my ears as pain stabs throughout my body. Spots explode across my vision. I wait for everything to calm and when it does, I try moving. Heavy rocks pin my leg down. Something digs into my back, but I don't know what it is. When I reach back, I feel something wet.

The screeching noise echoes in the sky. As I look to the dark night, dread fills my heart once I recognize the familiar shadow. It isn't one. It's several dragons. They're flying above, their shrill screams pierce through my ears. One of the dragons with deep green eyes opens its mouth shooting fire.

I duck hoping the rocks can shield me from the fire. The intense heat rolls over me, there is no relief in sight. Once the dragon stops, he moves on. When I raise my head, I scan the now blackened rocks and melted cell bars. To my left, I see an arm covered in blood with a gold sleeve.

Moving some rocks aside as best I can, I uncover Ena's face and notice the blue hue of her skin. A deep gash at her hairline bleeds down to her chin. I've never seen so much blood before and I try not to faint or throw up. Checking her pulse, I feel a faint heartbeat. I don't see Joffrey. I see a pile of rubble and dust all around me.

My hearing slowly returns as panicked screams and gunfire sounds in the distance. With each shot, I jump, feeling the anxiety creeping toward my heart. I sit for a moment, trembling, sucking in deep lungfuls of air. I have to get out of here. I have to find Casper. This isn't how I die.

"Is everyone okay?" I hear Nyx ask.

Florence and Fara respond. A few more down the hall slowly respond.

"Megan?" he asks.

"I'm okay. My leg." The pain is intense, and I hold back my cry. Unable to see, I push against the rock with my other leg, but it doesn't budge. I'm stuck and I try not to panic.

"We have to get out of here," Florence says.

Someone moans next to me, and they push rocks off them. I barely recognize Joffrey from all the dust and soot covering his face. Joffrey holds his head but once he notices the Queen, he climbs his way next to her.

"Queen Ena, wake up." He nudges her and removes more debris.

Ena moans as she opens her eyes. "What is happening?"

"Dragons are attacking," I tell her.

Surprise registers on her face, then it changes to something of acceptance. Perhaps realization that I was telling the truth.

She tries to sit up but cries out in pain. Joffrey cradles her in his lap. Ena's breaths come in short spurts. "Thank you, Joffrey."

"Your Majesty, we need to get out of here." He attempts to lift her up, but she stops him.

"No." Her amber eyes meet mine and she relaxes into Joffrey's arms. "You were right, Megan."

"What?"

A tear falls down her cheek, cleaning the dust from it. "Everything."

"Your Majesty, we need to get you to the safe place."

"No, Joffrey. You need to hear this as well. Megan was right about the Jewel."

Joffrey's face twists into confusion. "What?"

"The Jewel prevents Vincent from becoming a dragon. It's clear to me now that he and his father have decided to use his power against me. I never doubted you."

"What? Why did you fight me in front of everyone? Why did you lock me up? Are you only saying this because you're injured?"

Ena inhales a ragged breath. "I did not want anyone to know the truth. It's been kept hidden for many years. I feared if anyone knew, they would banish me."

"You imprisoned anyone who fought against you."

"I did. I never said I was perfect. I care deeply for the Elves and what is best for them. Unfortunately, I feared the truth being revealed someday. Deep down, I knew it was only a matter of time before it came out. Vincent's father is using Vincent against me. It has nothing to do with the Elves."

"What do you mean?" Joffrey asks, and we exchange a look.

"Why would they use it against only you?"

"Megan, if you are who you say you are, you can save us."

"I don't know how."

"You do. I know my son. He loves you and I know somewhere deep down inside you still love him. That's why I know you wouldn't kill him."

I gasp. "You're Vincent's mother?" Everything makes sense. Sort of. Why she never wanted to kill Vincent but wanted the Jewel. Why the war between the Elves and Sprites has become clear. It had nothing to do with Casper and me, yet, in a way it does. Vincent told me the truth.

Shame crosses her eyes. "I am. His father stole him away from me and threatened to use him against me. I never once sought him out for fear I would die. No one knew I had a baby. They all assumed he died at birth." Tears fill her eyes. "I have no doubt that Vincent believes I am a terrible person. Which, I am. The Elves need to know the truth. I fell in love with a Sprite."

Joffrey's face slowly falls, confusion sets in his eyes.

"All I cared about was power. After what his father did to me, I wanted to end the Sprites. I wanted them all to die. I was willing to do whatever it took in order to make that happen."

"You knew Vincent was a dragon all along."

She nods. "It was the greatest mistake of my life. His father cursed him." She shakes her head and grips my hand. "Megan, you must lead them to stop the war. Joffrey, you must help. I know I have no right to ask either of you for anything, but this war has to end."

"I agree."

"How did you find out? Did Vincent trust you with the truth, or what he thought was the truth?"

"The Jewel showed me visions of Vincent and his father. Rather, in the visions, *I* was Vincent. The Jewel led me right back to Vincent. I couldn't fight it. It controlled me."

She looks at me in a curious manner. "You and Vincent are bound together."

I shake my head. "No, we aren't. I want nothing—"

Ena raises her hand. "You and he are bound. Why do you think you've never been able to escape him all this time? Jacques must have used the witches to place a spell on you both at a very young age. That's why he trusts you and why he deeply loves you. It's the reason he was so cruel to you when you fell in love with Casper. That wasn't supposed to happen."

"But it did."

Ena nods. "It did. Yours and Casper's love is stronger than any spell. Stronger than any forbidden rule I could ever place on you both. Megan, you must be careful. Not everyone will be thrilled at the idea of you two together. I meant what I said about letting him go."

"Why?"

"It won't be easy for you, even if you kill Vincent. Being bound will affect you."

"If he dies, I'll die too?" I ask, frantic.

"No, but it will haunt you forever."

"Why would Jacques put a spell on Vincent and me?"

"To keep Vincent grounded and focused on what Jacques wanted. Jacques wanted your power as well, but Vincent cared for you so much, he erased it from your mind. So, Jacques did the next best thing and used Vincent's power. I'm positive that Vincent agreed to let his father use him as a pawn in order to leave you alone. You falling in love with Casper propelled Vincent into becoming a dangerous man."

"He can change though, can't he?" Am I truly the reason Vincent is a crazed man? Is it my fault for his behavior?

"Megan, you have to promise me to lead the Elves to safety. You and Casper. I never doubted your love. I could see it."

"Why all the theatrics?"

She swallows. "I never thought an Elf would love a Sprite or vice versa the way you two love each other. I never wanted another feud to break out between the two species. After my experience, I banished those who consorted with the enemies. I couldn't have such a quarrel happen again. You two can bring the Elves and Sprites together. In harmony. Only you two. You must fight for it. You must promise me this."

"But—"

"Promise me," she demands, lifting her head.

"Of-of course. I promise."

"Please accept my apologies, And you, Joffrey."

"Of course, madame."

She lays her head back down against Joffrey's chest and closes her eyes. I watch her shallow breaths for what seems like several minutes until her chest stops moving.

Twenty-Nine

dragon shrieks causing me to cover my ears. I wait for another blast of fire, but it doesn't come. I hear voices amplify as Joffrey wraps his arms around my waist attempting to lift me.

"Wait. The rock. It's pinning me down."

Joffrey pushes the rock off me and lifts me from the wreckage. "Let's get you to safety."

"Get away from her!" Casper shouts as he, Silvyr, and Zev rush into the dungeon.

"Casper." My heart feels as if it's going to burst through my chest. Tears pour down my face as I rush up to him as best I can, flinging my arms around him. I can't release him.

"It's okay," he whispers. "It's okay. We have to go."

Nodding, I draw back slightly. "Wait," I say. "We have to release the others."

"We have no time."

"No, Casper, we have to save them."

"I'm on it," Joffrey pulls out his keys and begins opening the cells. Once Florence is free, she hurries up to me, pulling me into a hug.

"We must hurry," Silvyr says.

Gripping Casper's hand, we climb out of the dungeon. As my gaze sweeps across the world, all I see is fire. Elves screaming and scrambling around in horror. Blood. There is so much blood. On the ground. On bodies. Bodies scatter across the ground, twisting in impossible positions. It's a nightmare. All of it. It can't be real. Nothing this horrific exists.

Casper holds my hand tight. In the dust and chaos, we hurry through the crowd. Fire burns trees, people, anything in its wake. I hobble along, my leg completely useless, trying to ignore the cries of the people. The dragons still loom above, their large bodies like shadows of death spraying fire everywhere.

I'm not sure how long it takes until we end up underground in a cave. The entrance is tall and as we make our way deeper, the air becomes cooler. The ground is muddy, and Casper holds me to make sure I don't fall down each time I slip. It seems like the cave belongs to the Elves and they use it as a refuge. As we make our way through, rocks jut out narrowing our path, then it opens up to a large room where several

Elves have taken shelter here. Clasping Casper's hand, I receive the familiar stares of hatred.

"Are we safe here?" Florence asks from behind.

Silvyr turns his head. "Very safe."

"No one will harm you. I assure you that," Joffrey says.

Zev scoffs. "Yeah, because you did a great job of that when they were in cells."

Joffrey turns to challenge him, even though Zev is twice his size. "I was following the Queen's orders. You would do the same if you cared about anything."

Zev shakes his head and walks past Joffrey.

I can't imagine what is going through Joffrey's head. Moments before, he learned his Queen had been lying all along to the Elves about the Jewel. The sole reason for the war. I'm still trying to wrap my head around everything myself. Vincent has turned into the dragon. Is he truly hopeless?

Once we reach a place in the cave, I collapse to the ground.

Casper kneels before me. "We have to fix your leg. I'm going to find Cyran."

He starts to stand, and I grab his shirt, pulling him to me. He kisses my forehead. "It's okay, Megan. It's okay." He kisses me once more, but I won't release him. Not yet.

I can't stop myself from trembling. I want to hold him as long as I can. I want to be sure it's real, that he's here with me.

Casper squeezes my hand. "Everything is okay. I promise. I will be right back." He gets to his feet and leaves.

Silvyr eases Florence onto the ground beside me. "Please forgive the horrible way the Queen has treated you. No angel should ever be locked up."

A small smile spreads across her face and she doesn't release his hand. "Thank you."

"Are you hurt? Do you need a medic?"

She shakes her head. "I'm okay." Florence turns to me and hugs me. "Thank you," she weeps. "You've saved my life. I owe you so much."

"It's okay now. You owe me nothing."

"What are they doing here?" a man cries as he points to Florence and me. "They are the enemies. They're the reason our village is burning. They should die for what they have done."

"Relax old man," Zev tells him. "They're on our side."

"They're Sprites! They don't belong here." He stares at me like I'm a disgusting rat. "She's the one who sent those dragons here."

"No, she didn't," Casper says.

"Of course, you would say that. You're a traitor."

I can't let this go on much longer. With my good leg, I use the wall to help me stand. "The Queen lied to you about the Jewel. About why you were warring with the Sprites. The Jewel isn't to keep you all alive. It's to keep Vincent from becoming a dragon."

"Clearly, that isn't the case," the old man spats. "Or did you forget the dragons that just annihilated our home?"

"I don't know how that happened. His father is controlling him."

The man shakes his head. "How dare you come into our home and spout such nonsense. You think anyone would believe anything *you* have to say? You're nothing but filth."

Casper slams his fist in the man's face. "They are no enemies. They're on our side." Zev and Silvyr pull him back.

The man spits in his face. "Traitor. Consorting with the enemy."

Another couple of men hold him back.

"Okay, okay we don't need any fights to break out." Cyran moves between them carrying a bag of medical supplies. "Just rest," he tells the angry man.

When Zev and Silvyr release Casper, Cyran makes his way to me. Of course, he's a doctor. He looks wise enough to be able to do anything. Like a medicine man.

Saida rushes over, wrapping her arms around Casper causing me to cringe. "You're okay."

"I'm fine. You?"

"It was a little dodgy." Her eyes rove over me. "Why are *they* here?" she whispers. "You know they are not welcome."

"Saida, stop. They are with me. Nothing will stop that."

She purses her lips in disapproval.

"Come on, jealous," Zev pulls Saida away from us.

"This may sting a little." Cyran gives me a shot of a pain killer and I wince a little, but the pain begins to subside. He starts assessing my leg.

How did Vincent find us? Had he always known where Belle Palais was, or did someone tell him how to get here?

When I look over to my left, there's an opening to the cave and from what I can see, it looks out over

Belle Palais. Flames reach the sky, and it breaks my heart to see all of the beauty, the homes, the people burning to death. Joffrey stands by the entrance. I have to talk to him.

Once Cyran wraps my leg, I stand.

"Megan, you should not be standing at all," he says.

"I'm okay."

Casper takes my hand. "What are you doing?"

"I need to talk to him." I hobble over to Joffrey and tap him on the shoulder. "Are you okay?"

He looks away, staring at the fires. "What do you think?"

"I am sorry."

Joffrey takes a deep breath. "Did you lead the dragons here?"

"No. I only knew of Vincent as a dragon. I had no idea there were others."

"She wanted you to steal the Jewel from Vincent."

"Yes."

"I never understood why we warred over that damn Jewel. I knew it didn't keep us alive or prevent us from aging. Now I wonder if some of our own kind were mysteriously killed by the Queen to keep the ruse going."

"I don't know."

"If the Jewel possesses you, how can you take it from Vincent?"

"I don't know."

Joffrey shakes his head. "I never thought in a million years that a Sprite would be helping us defeat the Sprites and possibly end the war."

"Trust me. I never thought any of this would happen either. For what it's worth, I didn't mean to cause any harm."

"For what it's worth, I didn't mean to as well. I'm sorry the Queen locked you up for telling the truth."

"Were you going to shoot me?"

He swallows. "Yes. Queen's orders. I have been trained never to hesitate. I have also been raised to despise your kind."

I nod, understanding.

"I must admit, from the moment you got here, I knew you were different than any other Sprite I encountered. You sympathize and I can tell you have been tortured. I know all about that torture."

"I'm sorry."

We stay silent for a few moments, then Joffrey turns around to face the crowd of wounded Elves. Casper stands next to me, letting me prop myself against him.

"We have lost our homes and our beloved Queen," he tells them, and a symphony of gasps echoes inside the cave. "We must defeat the Sprites and kill these dragons." They cheer. "As hard as it is to believe, these Sprites are on our side. No harm shall come to them and if any of you harm them, you will be punished. Truths have been told regarding the Jewel. Megan has spoken the truth."

Another round of gasps followed by whispers.

Joffrey holds up his hand. "I assure you it is true."

"She's manipulating you," a man yells from the back.

"The Queen herself told me the truth. Once we devise a plan and we are healed, we will attack the enemies. This war will end."

Cheers and applause vibrate within the cave.

Joffrey holds up his hand once again. "For now, we must rest." He returns to watching the fires and Casper helps me back to my seat.

"What are we doing? Where are we going?" Florence asks.

"Right now, we stay here," Silvyr says.

Casper kisses my forehead. "Are you okay?"

I nod. "I missed you." I press my hand to his face. "Did they hurt you? Did they torture you?"

"No, only the first day. The rest of the time, she tried to convince me that we didn't belong together and that they only way to free you was if we never saw each other again. I wanted you to be free. She wanted me to give you up. I told her I would."

"What?"

"Megan, your freedom is worth more. I couldn't be the reason you were in prison. I couldn't be the reason you couldn't live your life. I can't be selfish with you. Not like that."

Tears cloud my vision. "What would we have done? We never would've seen each other. Vincent would've captured me..."

He pulls me to his chest, holding me tightly. "It's okay, Megan. It didn't happen. So, the Queen admitted the truth?"

"Yes. She wanted me to lure Vincent and his army here so she could fight them."

"What?" Casper gives me a confused look.

"That's what she was going to do. Release me to find Vincent so she could get the Jewel."

Casper shakes his head. "I knew she was up to something. How did she expect you to get the Jewel from him without any help?"

I meet his eyes. "I have powers, Casper. I can make others see what I want them to see. I can make myself appear as anyone I want. She wanted me to use that against Vincent."

His jaw drops. "That's incredible."

"There's more, Casper."

"Like what?"

"The Queen told me other truths as well. About Vincent. About me."

"Okay." He looks uneasy and I don't blame him. I'm not quite sure how I feel about what I learned.

"She is his mother," I whisper.

He lets out a breath.

"She and Jacques have been fighting over the Jewel and Vincent in order to have the power of the dragons."

Casper doesn't respond, but he's thinking.

"She also told me," I swallow hard. "That Vincent and I are bound together. A witch placed a spell on us so that we would be together forever."

A crease forms between his eyes. "What?"

"Our love has proven to be stronger than any binding spell, that's why Vincent has lost it. That's what made him become so dangerous. This whole time he was taught to believe that he and I would be together, that it would help him. That I would always be his saving grace. He protected me from his father."

"What do you mean?"

"His father wanted to use me against the Elves and Vincent made me forget I ever had any sort of power and let his father use him instead."

"Does he know his parents are using him as a pawn in their own battles? Or to gain power?"

"No. He thinks his mother abandoned him, but she didn't. Jacques stole him from her, only she never could search for him."

"You almost want to feel sorry for him."

"While I'm thankful he protected me from his father, he always did things to benefit King Jacques. He's always wanted his father's approval and did everything he could to get it. I can't say it was to protect me, more as a means to please his father. King Jacques wanted the dragon."

"Why couldn't he see that his father's using him?"

I shrug. "Vincent's never had much, including a large family. He never knew his mom, his dad knew everything about him and kept it a secret, he feels he owes his father. He will always do what his father says because he needs that constant validation. Even though his father hardly ever gives it."

"What do we do?"

"I hate that I hurt Vincent, but I can't live like that. He will always choose his father and because I chose you, Vincent will never rest. He will always find us, even if his father is dead." I take a deep breath, hating what I'm about to say. "We have to kill him."

"Are you sure?" he asks, even though I know exactly what he wants to do.

"If we don't, it will only get worse."

He pulls me tighter to him and I rest my head on his shoulder. He intertwines our fingers. As he kisses the top of my head, I can feel his breath travel over my head. I'm relaxed but scared of what's to come. It won't be easy. It won't be good. Casper may never forgive me. I have to do whatever it takes to keep him safe. Even if that means he lives the rest of his life without me.

Thirty

The sun dips behind the horizon as I look out at the remnants of Belle Palais. Trees burned halfway down. Smoke drifts in the air as ashes fall like snow. The charcoal-like smell of charred flesh and the coppery metallic scent of blood clings to my nose. No matter what, I can't get rid of either. It hasn't left in several weeks.

The dragons fled around dawn or at least none of us have seen any. Perhaps the Sprites believe they killed all the Elves and left. Somewhere deep inside me knows that isn't the case. I never saw any Sprites, just dragons.

None of us slept. I didn't, even with Casper holding me. Every so often I would wake if I heard the slightest sound. Exhaustion weighs heavily over me, and I can't stop yawning. I hate what the Sprites did to Belle Palais. Our whole lives have been based around a lie. One lie that killed so many people. Prevented Casper and me from being together. I still don't know what Ena meant that I would never be free if I didn't let Casper go. Once the war ends and people learn the truth, we can be together.

"I used to come here as a child," Joffrey says, startling me. "My apologies." He stands next to me.

I let out a soft laugh. "It's okay. I'm a little jumpy lately."

He nods. "Understandable." He lets out a breath and gazes across the horizon. "It was certainly a sight to see at dark."

"Belle Palais was beautiful. It will be rebuilt."

"I admire your optimism." He looks at me. His pale green eyes, once fearful and young, have seemingly transformed overnight to older and more confident. I know witnessing a massacre like last night will do that to a person. I can't imagine what my eyes must appear like. Part of me doesn't even want to know.

"It hasn't been an easy thing to hold onto," I tell him, honestly.

"No, I suspect not."

We're quiet again for a few moments, enjoying the peace even if for just a moment.

"I know Queen Ena said not to kill Vincent. You saw what he did last night."

"I know. I don't know if King Jacques did something or if it was Vincent that made the decision."

"Megan, we have to end this. Destroying the Jewel won't be enough."

I nod. He's right. "What exactly did she mean that if I kill him, I'll be haunted?"

"Do you think you could use your magic to trick him?"

"I've worked this out in my head numerous times. I'm the only one who can get near Vincent. Sure, I can use my magic to appear as anyone, however Vincent will know."

"How? None of us could tell you were yourself."

"Since we are...bound." I swallow. The word burns in my throat. "He will be able to see through the magic. Just as I was able to see through his with the help of the Jewel. Now I know that's how he was able to hide it from me. Well, that and the fact that I was incredibly naïve. I let him make me believe anything."

"What if you appeared to be dead?"

"He would still see the truth."

"But you made us think Nyx was dead."

"You never checked his pulse though."

Joffrey purses his lips together in thought. After several minutes, he turns to me. "There may be another way."

"How?"

"There is a witch who makes elixirs so that you fall into a deep sleep, your heartbeat slows so much that it looks like you're actually dead. If Vincent thinks you're dead, we could bring your body to him. Once he sees you, in his moment of despair, we could strike. There is a time limit though."

I picture the Elves bringing my still body to Vincent and him grieving. Then I wake and stab him.

We can work out the details and for the first time in a while, I feel a little hopeful. The fear latches onto me. I've never killed anyone before, I don't know if I can. I know Casper is more than willing to kill Vincent, but he can't be seen. The second Vincent sees Casper, none of this will work.

Casper won't stay behind.

Maybe I can ask the witch to make two potions, so I can keep him safe.

"We can also bring Ena's body," I tell him. "Maybe seeing his mother will cause him to be more vulnerable."

Joffrey shakes his head. "No. She deserves to be buried here."

"Even after she betrayed us?" Silvyr walks up and joins us.

I place a hand on Joffrey's arm. "She won't be buried with the Sprites. This is just to lure Vincent to us."

Joffrey exhales. "We'd have to contact him to meet us."

"I can do that," Florence says from behind.

I turn around, shocked. "What? You can't be seen. They all think you're dead. He will kill you."

"No, he won't. I will tell him I've been a prisoner and that because of the dragons, I escaped. I will tell him that I made a deal with the Elves to bring yours and Ena's bodies to him for a proper burial."

I review it over in my head and Florence nudges me. It's good to see some of her spirit return. I don't want to risk her life. "Florence, you're safe now. You can go be happy. You've been tortured for years. Why do you want to do this?"

She puts her hands on my shoulders, her eyes holding mine. "You saved me. So now, I can save you and the Elves." I shake my head, but she squeezes my hand. "Megan, we can end this. For good. This will work."

"It's too dangerous," I say.

"Yeah, all of this is dangerous. It's the only shot we have. I have to do this. You all saved me. I have to repay you."

Silvyr frowns. "You do not need to repay us."

"This is what I'm doing."

"Then I will accompany you," Silvyr says.

"No. No Elves can be with me."

She can't be serious with this. "Florence, how will you be protected? How will he believe that you made a deal with the Elves?"

"We could set up a perimeter of an army," Joffrey says.

Florence shakes her head. "Vincent will be expecting that." She's right.

"Then let me accompany her." Nyx stirs from his spot.

"I don't need anyone to—"

"Just let Nyx help you."

She gives a pointed look. "Fine."

"What's going on?" Casper places his arm around me. I let him know our plan. He shakes his head. "Absolutely not."

"I have to."

"Do you think I'm going to let you walk into a death trap?"

"You don't have a choice. Vincent won't kill me. If he wanted me dead, he would've done it already. He wouldn't have let me die in those gallows."

"Megan—"

"Casper, I don't want to die. I'm not a martyr. I'm not the chosen one. It's just…both our sides have been at war for years because of Vincent. They're unknowingly keeping him safe. While his father controls everything and everyone. And if we don't do something, one day, it'll be Vincent to take his place. He has to die. This is the only way."

"You swear you can't use your powers?"

"Vincent needs to see my body and with the elixir, it will make my heartbeat faint. If I take the elixir, I won't be strong enough to use my magic, but I can kill him."

Joffrey nods. "Okay, so Florence leaves to tell Vincent that Megan and his mother are dead. We order a cease fire and agree on a meeting place. Then we bring yours and Ena's bodies to the meeting. So, how do you propose killing Vincent?"

"We'll hide a dagger. When I wake, I will stab him."

Casper shakes his head. "No. If you stab Vincent while there are Sprites, they will kill you."

"That's where the army comes in. You will not strike at the meeting place. You'll wait for us elsewhere. Once I kill him, that's when you strike."

"This is all going to depend on serious timing. We need to know how long the elixir lasts."

"We can get all the information once I see the witch."

"Casper and I will escort you," Joffrey says.

I nod. I need Casper to stay behind. He can't be there when I ask the witch for a sleeping potion for him. Perhaps I can ask Florence or Silvyr to help keep him behind. It has to come from them, otherwise, he will be suspicious.

"We'll head out in the morning," I tell them.

Casper grabs my hand. "You need to rest."

"I know." I don't argue as he pulls me to a secluded area of the cave. We lie down holding each other. I love these moments with him. Just us, in the dark, spilling secrets, or just being us. Like we're the only two people in the world.

"I can't believe this, Megan. You swear this plan will work?" he asks.

"Of course. It has to."

"I will be there every step of the way to make sure you're safe."

I nod but swallow the guilt that rises in my throat. I have to do this for him. I can't imagine a life without him.

He strokes my hair and I lean into his chest loving the feel of it. "I can't believe everything that's happened in the last few months."

"I know. It seems so long ago that we were dancing at the prom."

"Yeah. I loved that. You really miss our human life, don't you?"

"I do. I don't know why. It's like this intense pull, almost like I can't sever the tie or something."

He holds me closer. "Probably because we were taken away so fast, you never got to say goodbye to anyone."

"Once this is over, maybe I can return so that I can say goodbye. I do miss my mom and brother. Also, Cherry."

"I know. I wish I could return with you."

"It's okay."

We stay like that and the more I think about what's to come, I try to hold the tears inside, but they come out in quiet sobs. The pain fills my heart, and I can't breathe.

I don't want to leave Casper. I don't want to kill Vincent. I hope the plan works for everyone's sake. Including mine.

Thirty-One

It's still dark when I wake up. My eyes are raw and sting from the tears the night before. Also, from lack of sleep. Casper is still asleep next to me. I carefully untangle myself from him, grateful that he doesn't wake. I make my way to the cave opening and see Silvyr staring out.

"Everything okay?" he asks.

"Yes. Can't sleep. You?"

"Yes. Just thinking."

"Same."

"Anything I can help with?"

I let out a shaky breath. "Actually, I do need your help. Casper can't go with us to fight the Sprites. I have to stop him from fighting."

He narrows his eyes. "You know Casper will want to fight. Especially since he'll want to keep you safe. Why don't you want him with us?"

"Vincent thinks Casper is dead. The second he sees him he will kill Casper and know it was all a ruse. I don't know if I'll be fast enough."

"Casper said he would stay hidden with the army."

I shake my head. "He won't. I know the history between them. Once Casper sees Vincent, he will attack him."

He nods. "I have no doubt he will. We're all going in to kill Vincent and his father."

"I can't let Casper die."

"Don't you have faith in him that he will survive? Vincent has tried to kill Casper numerous times, yet he always survives."

"I don't have a good feeling this time. Yes, Casper has lived but every single time the two of them have fought each other, Vincent has won. He always had the upper hand."

"Now, we have the upper hand. He won't be expecting it. Why take away this revenge for Casper?"

I meet Silvyr's eyes. "This isn't Casper's revenge. Killing Vincent is mine," I blurt. The words shock me for a moment. "He's caused so much pain and heartache. This is what I must do. For myself. For Casper. For everyone who has died by Vincent's hand."

Silvyr studies me for a moment.

"I want to keep Casper safe."

"And what is it that you need me to do?"

"On the day of the attack, I'm going to inject the same potion I'm taking into him. It will put him to sleep. I need you to keep him safe somewhere. Where no one will find him. If this plan doesn't work and the Sprites attack, he will need to be alive."

Silvyr shakes his head. "You're going to drug him? How do you propose you do that?"

"I don't know yet. I'm going to ask the witch for two potions. I have to do this, Silvyr. I know it's a lot to ask."

"He won't be happy with this. When he wakes, if you are not here, I will have lost his friendship. He won't forgive you."

"No, he won't but he'll be alive. He means too much to me."

"What if you die? Then he will wake, blame me, and will have to live out his days miserable and alone."

"I know. Nothing about this makes me happy. It's the only way I can keep him alive. You must not tell anyone where he's kept."

"Megan, that's assuming I will do this. I should tell him—"

"No, please. Please, you have to help me."

"I will think about it."

"Thank you." It's all I can hope for at this point. "There's one more thing."

He lifts an eyebrow.

"Tomorrow we are to get the serum from the witch. I also plan to get the potion for Casper. I need you to keep him here. He can't come with me. He can't know that I'm getting two doses of the potion."

"Don't you think he would rather save you than himself? He would die for you."

"I know that. He's tried many times. I need to do this for him. I love him and he's saved me so many times. It's my turn to save him. Once I administer the potion, I don't know how much time he'll have. I'll explain it to him, and I will make sure he won't blame you. None of this is on you. It's me."

Silvyr nods. "I appreciate that."

"Will you do it?"

"I have yet to decide."

I nod.

"I do have one question, if you don't mind."

"Go ahead."

"Why are you risking your life for the Elves? I know you love Casper but what about the rest of us. They treated you so poorly. The Queen locked you up for several weeks. She admitted the truth to you and that she'd lied, yet still you want to help us?"

"I am not a vindictive person. Whatever the Elves did to me was because of fear of the truth being exposed. It had nothing to do with me. I may be a little vindictive toward Vincent, though."

"Deservedly so."

I still don't want to kill anyone. "This isn't all about me or the Elves. I'm also hoping to save my people as well. Save them from the manipulation of Jacques. If Vincent becomes the dragon again, everyone will die. You saw what the dragons are capable of doing. Jacques will not stop controlling Vincent until every single Elf is dead, this also goes for Sprites. I have seen them torture innocent Sprites, for what they deem is betrayal. They sent several innocent men to their deaths."

"What was their supposed crime?"

I shake my head, as if trying to remove the sound of the crowd when those men were beheaded. "Jacques took over the kingdom yet refuses to care for its people. He only cares about himself and taking over the world. He would take a wife for himself each night and if the husbands refused, the King would hang them. They were scared to say anything or revolt against the King. He threatened me."

Silvyr's eyes widen. "How long has this been happening?"

"Years. At least since Casper and I have been in the human world."

He nods in understanding. "Wow. I had no idea."

"He convinced my parents to disown me."

He squeezes my hand. "I'm sorry to hear that."

"None of the Sprites know the truth of the Jewel. What few people are in this cave know, that's it. They should know what they've been fighting for all these years. They need someone to help them."

"We've been warring with the Sprites for centuries over that damn Jewel. I always had an inkling that it had some other meaning." He shakes his head. "What happens once we kill Vincent?"

"Then we must go after Jacques. Although, I suspect he will be right beside Vincent. Once the two of them are dead, the Sprite Kingdom will have no leader. I will return and show them the truth."

"How are you going to get them to listen? Especially to you, Megan? Aren't you considered a traitor to them?"

I let out a sigh. He's right and I don't know how I will make the Sprites listen. "I spoke to a few of the villagers. Something tells me that if the tyrant dies, they will be relieved. If I provide them comfort and food and give back their lives, they will believe me."

"I fear that killing Vincent will not stop this war, especially if the army fights with Vincent and King Jacques no matter what. They have a king to serve and will have to abide by those rules. It will only ignite it."

"Not if we kill Jacques or take him hostage. The army will surely surrender."

"Don't be naïve. The army has fought against us for centuries. They won't stop fighting."

"We have to try. If we take Jacques as our prisoner and force him to tell the Sprites the truth, they will understand."

Silvyr purses his lips. "We could. What would compel him to tell the truth?"

I shrug. "Maybe seeing his son dead. He has no power without Vincent. This plan will work. It has to." Everything must fall into place. We deserve that much. I wipe away stray tears and peer out at the blackened ruins of the castle on the hill. Smoke still billows into the dark sky.

"It will," Florence says from behind us.

I freeze. "I didn't think anyone was listening."

"It's okay."

Silvyr turns to her. "And you. You're willing to risk your life for this as well?"

"Of course. I was in love with Edmond, and he would have done the same for me."

He shakes his head. "Even after we have kept you prisoner for all those years?"

"If the war ends, no one will be prisoner. With Casper and Megan together, they can lead both of us to a greater future." She exchanges a look with me.

"I admire your bravery," Silvyr says.

Florence smiles and shyly looks away.

"Casper will stay safe?" I ask him.

Silvyr takes a deep breath and studies me. "You have my word that Casper will remain safe."

Relief floods through me and warm tears fall. "Thank you."

"You're welcome," Silvyr says, and retreats.

Florence hugs me. "I promise this will work and Casper will be safe. We will all be happy one day."

"I hope so." Hugging her reminds me of Cherry and part of me feels guilty because I feel like I'm closer to her than I am Florence. I don't know what it is.

When she pulls away, she smiles and meets up with Silvyr. The two of them are cute. I can sense they like each other, and I know it will take Florence some time to move on from Edmond.

As I peer out into the night, I have a strong feeling this will be the last time I see everyone, including Casper. The devastating emotion has wedged itself deep inside me. I slowly and quietly let it escape. I know Casper will never forgive my betrayal, perhaps he will understand more than I think. We are saving innocent people and will hopefully end the war. I wish it didn't have to come at the expense of someone dying, especially by my hand.

I feel warm, strong arms wrap around me and breathe a sigh of relief. He makes me feel safe and comfortable. I feel guilty. For lying to Casper. For tricking Vincent.

"Are you okay?" he asks.

I nod.

He turns me around to face him and with his thumbs he wipes away my tears. "Don't be scared, Megan. We will succeed."

"I don't want to think about it tonight. I want you and me right now."

"Come with me." He takes my hand and leads me away from the cave until we reach a private wooded area. It's quiet and dark. Part of me fears seeing a dragon but they've been gone.

"Casper," I say, a little uneasy about making out in the woods when anyone could see us.

"Look up at the sky."

It's darker here and within seconds, I see the shower of stars across the sky. He kisses my neck and immediately, I melt in his arms.

"I've never seen a meteor shower before."

"Neither have I. I'm glad it's with you."

"It feels a little surreal. Being here with you. Watching a meteor shower. I never thought this would happen."

He squeezes me tighter. "It's real. It's the realist thing I've ever felt. You are my happiness." He presses his lips against mine, slipping his tongue to meet mine. Fire ignites deep inside me as he tangles his hand through my hair.

I can't get enough of him, and I never want these moments to end.

But I know they have to.

Thirty-Two

Nerves assail my stomach and I feel sick. I've been awake for a few minutes, trying not to freak out. Casper and I made love last night and fell asleep. It was beautiful and he was gentle as always. I hate the feeling of impending doom that hovers over me. The same feeling I had right after I saw the dragon.

I inhale a breath and slowly let it out. I have to see the witch.

I nudge Casper and he moans. He opens his eyes, that beautiful brown staring back at me. I love the color. I love how that smoldering look always draws me in. Unable to resist, I press my lips to his and he rolls on top of me.

"I love you, Megan," he whispers.

"I love you."

He kisses me, chaotic and urgently. Needing me as much as I need him, unsure if we'll ever have this again. We give in to our urges, satisfying that intense craving we need.

"We should get back."

Casper pulls his shirt over his head. "Guess it's time to see the witch."

Hand in hand, we return to the cave, while I try to swallow the guilt.

"Where have you been?" Joffrey asks. "We have been worried about you."

"I'm sorry," Casper says. "It was my fault. Are we ready?"

"Someone has to stay here to be in charge."

Casper nods. "Okay. Megan and I will handle the witch."

"I think it would be best if you stayed. If anything happens, it's best if you two aren't seen together."

"What are you talking about?"

"If we encounter any Sprites and they see the two of you together, they will know she's with us. If they see me with her, we can pretend she's my prisoner."

"He's right," I tell him. "Word would get back to Vincent and then our plan wouldn't work."

"Or worse, they'll kill you both on the spot," Joffrey says.

Casper shakes his head and turns to me. "I don't like this."

"Unfortunately, we don't have much of a choice."

"Why don't you and I go instead?" he asks Joffrey.

"One of us has to stay here to keep the Elves in check. We can't have them starting something with the Sprites who are on our side. They already don't like that there are several with us. I assure you that I will keep her safe."

Casper studies him. "Can I trust you with her?"

"Of course."

"You have to admit that I don't like this at all. You didn't help her when she was a prisoner."

"It's okay." I touch Casper's arm, meeting his eyes. "I trust Joffrey. He was only protecting his Queen."

"I apologize for my part in hurting you."

"It wasn't your fault," I tell him. "We'll be okay, Casper. I promise."

He gathers me in his arms. "Please be safe, Megan." He lips meet mine and kisses me fervently.

Joffrey clears his throat, and we pull apart.

"I'm ready," I tell him.

He nods and we leave the cave. We are both trusting our lives with each other, which I guess we have been this whole time. I can't imagine how he's feeling or what he's going through emotionally.

Ashes from the fires fall over us like snowflakes. If only it were snow. Fall is approaching, and I know there won't be any beautiful foliage this season, given that the trees are completely burned, like most of this land.

I come to a halt. The enchanted forest I encountered before. With all the bodies and the trees, dead. Dragons destroyed it.

"What is it?" Joffrey asks as he stops and turns around.

"The dragons. They've damaged everything."

"Yes. Do we know who the other dragons are or where we can find them?"

I match my pace with Joffrey as we move deeper into the scorched forest. The further we walk, the more I see how much more obliterated the forest is. I wonder if the witch is still alive. What if the dragons destroyed her, too?

"I'm not sure. Ena only mentioned Vincent."

"Think he or Jacques will tell us with the right amount of torture?"

"Maybe. I've never known him as a prisoner."

"He certainly has put enough of us in the cells. I suppose so have we." He gives me an embarrassed glance and smirks. "It wasn't fair of the Queen to arrest you."

I shrug. "I wasn't right in how I approached the situation. I was angry and desperate for her to believe me. I *needed* someone to believe me, given the dire situation."

"I understand now just how dire. You spend your entire life believing something, always striving to keep going in that direction, then all of a sudden, you learn that it was all wrong. Everything you ever knew or believed. Vanished in the matter of seconds. Part of me feels like a fool for believing in it. I'm still struggling with the truth."

"As am I. Joffrey, don't ever feel like a fool for how someone manipulated you into thinking a certain way. The important thing is that you know the truth and you're working toward a better future."

"I'm trying."

"It isn't easy. Vincent has spent years controlling me. Making me think things about myself that weren't true. Making me feel things I never thought I could. He reeled me in, told me everything I wanted to hear, he wanted a puppet to control. He tried turning me against my friends and family. Even my dreams. He didn't care unless it benefited him."

"That's terrible."

"I have struggled with it for some time. Always believing it was my fault. That I'm a bad person or that I'm not good enough. No matter what I did or how I acted, it was never enough for him. It was like walking on broken glass. It took me a long time to realize it was him and his mind games."

"All these lies started with his family. This entire war is rooted with their lies."

"I know."

"You're an incredibly regal and humble person. I admire your strength."

I give a soft laugh. "I just do what I can to get through."

"Exactly. You don't give up. You have a tenacity. Fit for a queen. You can lead these people to greatness."

"I don't know about that. I can't stand aside and let someone take over like that. I can't stand by while someone kills innocent people. It isn't right."

"No, it isn't. It's been going on for far too long."

"I tried talking Vincent into becoming a better king. I'm sure he will do exactly as his father did."

We fall into silence as we continue the path. The ashes stop falling once we reach a part of the forest that has been untouched by dragons. I never thought I would see green again. The smell of pine overwhelms me, and I welcome it. I breathe it in as much as I can.

As night falls, we stop near a brook. In the distance, I can barely make out snowcapped mountains that glisten under the moonlight. It's beautiful here and reminds me of the cabin Casper and I stayed in during one of our human lives. I remember looking out on the deck at the vast mountain range, awing such beauty. It was chilly and Casper came outside wrapping a blanket around me as we gazed at millions of stars. I had never seen a sky full of stars like that before. Being in the city, it was difficult to see such an array. It was like seeing the entire galaxy.

Joffrey builds a fire. I used to love the smell of campfire but after smelling the forests, it makes me sad. He keeps his rifle close to his body, and still wears his uniform, while I'm still in the what-used-to-be-white cotton dress. I long for something else to wear but everything has been burned. There is a slight chill in the air tonight and I'm not going to be able to sleep. Every pop or crackle of the fire makes me jump and I look out into the darkness.

"A little jumpy, yeah?" he asks.

"A little. I can't help it."

He nods. "Trauma will do that. I get that way sometimes. War." An emotion appears across his eyes for a second, but he evades my stare.

"I am sorry for all you have lost."

"Thank you. You as well."

"Vincent made me think the war was because of Casper and me."

"No. You know that's not true."

"I never meant to leave my family or friends behind."

"No, you had to. Don't let Vincent make you feel like any of this was your fault. Don't let him make you think he's good."

I nod.

"What exactly did the witch do for you and Casper?"

"She created a way for us to be together. She made us human and let us experience several lifetimes together as humans. We've not been able to be ourselves here."

"We're changing that. We'll make it happen."

"Thank you. For everything."

"Don't thank me yet."

"Sometimes I wish we could go back to the human world."

"Why is that?"

I shrug. "I'm not sure. I just miss it. This last one in particular."

"Tell me about it."

As I start to tell him, a rustling in the trees prompts me to jerk my head toward the sound. My heart slams to my chest. Something or someone is out there.

"What is it?" Joffrey whispers.

"Someone is out there."

"I think it's your mind playing tricks. I don't see anything."

A pop sounds and I feel a bullet whiz by my face. It hits the tree behind me. Joffrey stands alert. I hurry behind a tree.

"We have to leave," I tell him.

Another shot.

"Show yourself, coward," Joffrey shouts.

Five men wearing black Sprite uniforms saunter from the darkness. Their guns drawn at us. My pulse edges higher. We did not come all this way only for them to capture us. I refuse to be a prisoner again. I wish I had a gun so I could help Joffrey.

Holding up my hands, I reveal myself from behind the tree. "We mean no harm."

One of the guards stares right at me. He recognizes me.

I know we only have one shot at this. Joffrey must kill all of them before they return to the Sprites.

"Put down your weapon," the man demands Joffrey. "You're outnumbered."

I move in front of Joffrey. "You have to shoot," I tell him as softly as I can and without moving my lips much.

"On my command, move."

"Drop your weapon," they demand once more.

"Move!" Joffrey shouts and I duck behind the tree. Shots are fired and something lands at my feet. A gun.

I snatch it up and fire toward the guards. I don't even know if I hit anyone. The smoke from the gunfire clouds my vision.

Then it's quiet.

Once the smoke fades, I see five dead Sprites and Joffrey on the ground wincing in pain. My hand trembles as it still holds the warm gun. I've never felt such power and fear all at once. I killed someone. I've never shot a gun before; I don't like it. I feel so ashamed of myself.

But I had to. I had to shoot them. They were going to take us or worse, kill us. They are the bad guys. It isn't true though. How can they be bad if they are following orders? Aren't they innocent like the rest of the Sprites?

"Megan." Joffrey's voice is muffled, and I can't catch my breath. I feel as if we ran through the forest for miles. I didn't even use my powers to help. I didn't even think. How could I have done nothing? Why couldn't I think of something? Why didn't I do something? I stood there.

"Megan!"

I snap my attention toward him and gasp as blood pours out of his leg. "Joffrey. Are you okay?"

"Just a flesh wound. You?"

"I-I'm fine."

Grabbing a sash from one of the dead soldiers in my shaky hands, I rush to Joffrey and lay the gun beside me. I wrap the sash around his bleeding leg cutting off the circulation.

He chuckles.

"What? Did I wrap it wrong?"

"Just ironic that a sash from my enemy is what's saving me."

"Oh. We need to get you back to see the doctor."

"No, Megan, we must finish this."

I let out a sigh. How stupid were we to not bring an army? Did we think Sprites wouldn't be scouring this land? Did we think we were safe? That the Sprites had left? As I kneel beside Joffrey, these thoughts attack my mind.

"Megan, we have to keep moving."

"Why didn't we bring an army?"

"Because it would've brought too much attention. You know that. If they only see two of us, they won't think anything more than a stroll. You have to help me to my feet."

I hear the faint sounds of horses whinnying. Grabbing the gun, I jump to my feet and run toward the sound.

"Megan!" I hear Joffrey call, but I have to bring a horse to him.

The gun weighs heavily in my hand, ready to fire. My heart beats like rapid gunfire as I near five black horses all tied to trees. Removing three of the saddles and reigns, I free them. The other two, I untie from the tree and lead them back to Joffrey. One of them nickers as they move with me.

Joffrey leans against the log and points his gun. He lowers it when he sees me. "You shouldn't have done that."

"Now we have horses. This will help us get to our destination quicker."

Joffrey struggles to get to his feet, and I wince as he puts pressure on his hurt leg. I help him as much as I can to get him on the horse. He lets out a few screams, and once he's on the horse, he lets out a deep breath.

I mount my horse. "Are you sure we shouldn't go back?"

"Megan, we'll make it. Come on."

Nudging the horse with my heel, we start galloping through the forest. I remember when Casper and I did this to see the witch. That was when she gave us the elixir to make us human. Feels like forever ago, yet again I'm racing in the night to save our lives.

hold me once again.” She likes me to see her. “You
know me now. Is this a new low?” she asks me.

I shake my head. “No. Gods are safe.”

His eyes rove over Gracie's bleeding leg. His
wrinkled lips purse together in thought.

“We've found a way so that the wards” continue,
until she pukes again. “Rises. Wait.”

The water is more very well for someone who
looks to be dragging. No hand has had back. Nothing
bit came. Perhaps. It's all for show. Maybe she's my
aunt. The woman squints with a bottle of the liquid a
towel, and a vial. “Drink this pill through.” Drink
this. She gives it in the liquid.

Something about the way she carries herself or
the tone in her voice, or the fear I may not. I hesitate
when she tells a child something. Once there, she

Thirty-Three

The witch's cabin hasn't changed one bit. It's a small hut in the middle of the forest and looks abandoned. As Joffrey and I enter, it's enormous. I remember the hundreds of clocks ticking at different times. The thousands of vials and bottles filled with translucent green, purple, blue, and yellow liquids. Flickering candles are placed anywhere there is room. Scents of oranges, sage, eucalyptus, lavender, sandalwood, and vanilla mix in a strange concoction. I can't decide if I like it or if it's too strong.

An old woman with long white hair emerges from behind curtains. She studies me for a long while until recognition flashes in her grey eyes. "You have found me once again." She moves to see Joffrey. "You, I do not know. Is this a new love?" she asks me.

I shake my head. "No. Casper is safe."

Her eyes rove over Joffrey's bleeding leg. Her wrinkled lips purse together in thought.

"We've found a way to end the war," I continue but she walks away. "Please. Wait."

The woman moves very well for someone who looks to be over ninety. No hunched back. No limps. No canes. Perhaps it's all for show. Maybe she's my age. The woman returns with a bottle of blue liquid, a towel, and a vial with two pills inside.

"Take these," she hands the pills to Joffrey. "Drink this." She gives him the liquid.

Something about the way she carries herself or the tone in her voice, neither Joffrey nor I hesitate when she tells us to do anything. Once he does, she removes the sash from his leg. We watch in amazement that his wound seals and heals itself.

"The pain will subside in a few minutes," she tells him.

"Thank you, ma'am."

The witch waves her hand like healing his leg wasn't a big deal and sits behind a wooden table. She invites us to sit across from her. "Please. Enlighten me on how to end the war."

"Vincent, the one we've been running from this whole time, is a dragon. There are more dragons, and they annihilated the Elves and their land." I rush through my words. "If I can trick Vincent into thinking I'm dead, I can get close enough to him to kill him for good."

"He found you in the mortal world, didn't he?"

I swallow hard. "Yes."

"Can you help us?" Joffrey asks.

"Of course, I can. I am a very powerful witch. This elixir you speak of will take days to make."

Joffrey and I exchange a worried look.

"How many days?" he asks.

"Usually, a week because I have to collect the ingredients and it has to stew for hours."

"What if we help you find the ingredients?"

"You could. How will you kill Vincent?"

"When I wake, I plan to stab him with a dagger."

The witch stands and rummages through several drawers. She pulls out a dagger and a vial from a shelf and hands them to me. The dagger is smaller than I expected with a long silver blade. The handle is black with silver lines around it. The vial is filled with a fine blue sand-like grain.

"Before you stab him, dip the dagger in this," she says. "This is a dragon killer. There is no cure, either."

She's so nonchalant about it, like killing dragons is a natural occurrence. Like killing bugs. "Thank you."

"May I ask why you are so willing to help us?" Joffrey asks. "I mean without question you healed my leg. You aren't even afraid of us."

The corners of her mouth turn upward in a knowing smile. "I am a very powerful witch. No one can attack me, if they try, I will defeat them."

"Then why haven't you ended the war yourself?" I don't miss the offended tone in his voice.

"This is not my war."

"How can you say that? How have you not been affected by it?"

"I've seen this war rage on for centuries, only a very few know I exist. I do not belong to either side, nor will I ever."

"Yet you're helping us end the war."

"I am helping both sides end the war because it is the right thing to do. I have been waiting for the right person to approach me for help. They have. I helped them in return to figure out a way to end this. Besides, I am not ending the war with this elixir you ask me to make. I am simply aiding. The rest is for you to figure out."

"We greatly appreciate your help," I tell her.

"Always. Is there anything else I can do?"

I clear my throat. "Actually, yes. I need a sleeping potion."

"A sleeping potion?"

"Yes. Casper cannot be present when we attack Vincent." I can feel Joffrey's eyes on me. "If Vincent sees him." I shake my head. "It won't be a good idea for Casper to be there. I plan to put him to sleep long enough for us to kill Vincent and return. Then we will gather the army and return to Château de Fées and explain the truth."

The witch gets up again and returns with another vial of orange liquid. "This is a truth serum. Give this to Jacques. I take it Queen Ena has left this world."

"How did you know?" Joffrey asks.

"I know more than you think. The way Jacques and Vincent have treated the Sprites is wrong."

Joffrey's jaw twitches. "How can you know these things and not get involved?" His voice rises and I know he is trying to keep it level. He's clearly frustrated.

"Again, this is not my war. I only do things if I know it will be good. I cannot help one side and not the other. If everyone knew I existed, they would ask me to do everything for them. I only perform such tasks on those I deem worthy."

"What if someone approaches you who isn't worthy?"

"They don't have that option. If I do not want someone to find me, they cannot."

"You hide from everyone?"

"I have not moved in centuries. I remain in the same place. I know who is coming, if I do not want them to see, I do not reveal myself."

"Doesn't that get lonely?"

"Never." The witch gives a smile like there's something more to her answer.

"Had Megan not been with me, would you have revealed yourself to me?"

The witch studies him. "Yes. You are a worthy man who has recently learned the truth about the Nuummite Jewel. You are conflicted, yet you know what must be done."

"How do you know so much about me?"

"I am a good reader of people. Now, let me get you that sleep potion, dear. It will take five minutes to take effect and will last up to an hour." She leaves once again and returns with a bottle. "Now, I have a syringe or capsule to give this to Casper."

I squeeze my hands together. "I-I guess a syringe."

She hands me a needle. "Fill it all the way. Inject it into a vein."

Holding the syringe, tears spring to my eyes. I hate that I'm even thinking of doing this to Casper. What have I become? A liar. A killer. A monster.

"Oh dear. It's okay. It won't kill him."

"That's not why she's crying," Joffrey says.

"You're afraid you won't make it back."

I wipe the tears from my cheeks. "It is a fear, yes."

"Be strong. You are not a bad person for doing this. You are saving lives. You are doing good."

I nod, trying my best to believe her, however I don't see how I am any better than Vincent right now. "How long does the semivivus last?"

"It depends on how long you need it to last."

Joffrey and I exchange a look. "An hour?"

"This has to be exact," Joffrey says. "As in, we will have timers, so no matter if you've killed Vincent by a certain time, we will attack the rest of his group."

"How long will it take me to be cognizant?"

"Five minutes."

"I think that'll be fine."

Joffrey nods. "Okay."

"I will start gathering ingredients. You two are welcome to join me or stay here."

"I'm up for an adventure," Joffrey says with a smile. "You?"

"Sure."

We follow the witch through a back door, and I gasp. It looks nothing like what we saw when we arrived.

This place is beautiful with wheat fields on one side and seemingly miles and miles of bushes and flowers and trees. The sky is perfectly blue, and the sun isn't too hot. A slight breeze sails through. I catch hints of peonies and wisteria and yellow broom flowers that emit a sweet smell of honeysuckle.

The further we walk, I see rows and fields of boldly fragrant lavender, brightly colored sunflowers, and perfectly manicured cypress trees.

It's incredible and it's no wonder the witch keeps it a secret. If I were her, I would, too.

We spend the day gathering berries from Lily of the Valley plants, chamomile flowers, lavender, and unusual flowers and herbs that aren't familiar to me. When we return to the witch's home, we help her prepare the ingredients by stripping leaves, crushing berries, and chopping flowers. It's a lot of work. Afterward, I feel like we prepared dinner for several people. My hands have all kinds of strange fragrances and no matter how many times I wash them, I can't get rid of the scent. Though it's better than smelling blood.

While the potions cook, the witch sets Joffrey and me up in a small room with a fireplace and some cushions and blankets in front of it. I want to curl up in the corner and sleep.

"How did you find her?" Joffrey asks, poking the fire.

"Casper found her ages ago. I'm not sure how."

"I can't believe I never knew she existed." As he continues to stir the fire, I realize something is on his mind.

"What is it?"

"I can't believe all of this is happening and that it's true. I'm questioning my loyalty."

"Don't do that. Your loyalty should remain with the Elves. Perhaps when this is over, loyalty will be to each of us."

I let out a breath. "Honestly, Vincent is so brainwashed by his father. He only knows that Elves are evil and that they will always be evil until every last one is dead."

"I am curious as to how you fell for an Elf over a Sprite. You loved Vincent, yeah?"

"I did. When I met Casper, I was drawn to him. Something about him was different and the more time we spent together, the more I didn't want to be apart. I knew what would happen and I broke Vincent's heart. Since then, I've come to know who Vincent is. He's dangerous and manipulative and will do anything to get what he wants."

"Do you think Vincent would've turned into this person had you not met Casper?"

I think about it for a few minutes. After seeing Jacques control him with that Jewel and everything else, I know Vincent would be. "Yes. He's very impressionable, at least when it comes to his father. He claims he can't rebel against his father because of everything he has done for him."

"Such as?"

"His father kept his true identity a secret. No one knows he's part Sprite and Elf. If they knew, they would kill him and his father."

"Why didn't you tell the Sprites the truth?"

I let out a dry laugh. "No one would have believed me. Especially with King Jacques threatening to kill anyone who went against his word. I'm the one rumored to have willingly escaped with an Elf. The

King squashed those rumors and vowed he would punish anyone who brought them back. He only kept Vincent's secret because he wanted to use his power. That's the only reason."

"Vincent never believed that?"

"No. Somewhere deep inside, he truly believes he owes his father. He has always believed his mother abandoned him and wanted nothing to do with him."

"His father has manipulated him his entire life, yeah?"

"Yes. He was also able to manipulate the Sprites. The way they are now." I shake my head. "And they call me the traitor."

Joffrey squeezes my hand. "We will fix all this. It won't be easy, but we will accomplish this."

I nod. "How did you know I couldn't let Casper accompany me on this trip?"

"A soldier never sleeps, I suppose. I overheard your conversation last night with Silvyr." He gives a sheepish grin. "I apologize. It was wrong; however, I agree with you."

"You do?"

"I know Casper doesn't trust me with you and I also understood where you are coming from. I had a love once. She lived in the villages, and I never wanted her to become part of this. As in part of the army. I knew it would be too hard for us to say goodbye every time I deployed. Then they made me a guard of the prisoners. Not exactly proud of that position."

"Do you know the fate of your girlfriend?"

Joffrey frowns and lowers his head. "No."

"We should look for her."

"I'm not sure she would want to see me."

"Why wouldn't she?"

He shrugs. "It's late. You should get some rest."

Maybe when this is over, we can search for her. I feel like something else happened, but I don't want to press him.

"Thank you for your help, Joffrey. And for believing in me."

"Of course. You're welcome."

Something nudges me and I wake with a start. An old woman stands over me. The witch. It takes me a second to remember seeking her out to make a potion. I must have been in a deep sleep.

I rub my eyes and notice Joffrey sleeping in an uncomfortable position.

"Your serum is finished," the witch says.

"Already?"

"You and Joffrey helped. Takes a lot less time when there are multiple people making it. I put all your goodies in a bag." She holds it up proudly. "The bag is indestructible, so if you run into any trouble, the bottles will not break. Also, if someone else steals the bag, the potions will explode."

"Thank you." I take the bag from her. "How can we pay you?"

"Your money is no good here. End this war once and for all."

I prod Joffrey's shoulder and he opens his eyes reaching for his gun. "It's me," I say.

When his wide eyes meet mine, he relaxes. "My apologies. Old habits."

I wave him off. "Are you ready?"

"That's it? Did we pay?"

"I already told her your money is no good here."

Joffrey stands. "Thank you for your generosity and shelter, among everything else." He salutes her.

"Don't mention it. Good luck."

"Thank you," I tell her.

We step outside under the grey dawn. The air is cool as the sun barely crests the horizon. The land is barren and sad. I miss the beautiful gardens we strolled through yesterday.

We hoist ourselves onto the horses and head back to the cave.

The woods are dark and eerie, almost in a haunting way. A low, thick fog surrounds us making it difficult to see in front of us. We slow our pace.

"I can't see a thing. It wasn't like this yesterday."

"Be on the lookout," Joffrey says. "Stay close to me."

I watch all around me. My hearing is amplified. A bird flutters its wings as it departs a tree. Something moves in the short distance to my right. I slow to a stop. Trees are broken. Limbs and leaves are strewn all over the forest floor.

"What is it?"

"Something's not right."

"Keep moving."

Squinting through the fog, I notice something large rise and fall. "Is that a bear?"

It breathes out, clearing some of the fog and its tail moves.

I freeze.

"Megan, we must leave."

But I can't move.

It's a dragon. Black scales. Two horns protrude from its head behind the ears, a third is centered on its head. Large nostrils breathe in the fog and push it away at every exhale.

I could stab it right now, but I don't know if it's Vincent. Are the other dragons nearby? I don't know what to do. I pray the horses don't whinny or make any other sound.

Slowly reaching in my bag, I try to find the dagger. If I'm careful enough, we could end it all right here.

"Megan, no. It's too risky," Joffrey says, his voice low.

The beating in my chest makes my ears throb. I can end it all right now.

"Megan." Joffrey grabs my arm.

I gasp.

The dragon opens its eyes.

Thirty-Four

Golden yellow irises with an oblong pupil hold my gaze, as if freezing me into place. I tell myself to move. Nothing happens. The horse neighs, and the dragon's eyes shift. Its black scaly body shudders as it rises high into the sky. I have to crane my neck to see its head. The dragon spreads its wings wide and full. As the sun shines through, I can see the web of veins, making the wings appear tenuous. If I weren't scared out of my mind, I'd probably admire the beauty of the dragon.

"Megan!" Joffrey shouts and my horse takes off.

Fast, through the fog laden forest. Darting to miss this tree and that. The cool air whipping my hair. I don't dare look back. I don't need to see the dragon watching us. The ground shakes as it takes a step and

I hear trees snapping and falling behind me. The horses neigh and speeds up. My heart matches their hasty pace.

"We must find shelter," Joffrey says. "We can't lead them to our cave."

Up ahead, I notice we're coming to the end of the forest. "We have to abandon the horses. Whoa." I slow my horse down and jump off. Slapping her behind, I send her away, hoping she will be safe. Joffrey follows and we run to the left of the woods.

As I run, I scan everything for shelter. Pointing to what appears to be a bunker, Joffrey nods. The dragon screams, the sound is earsplitting. Fire escapes its mouth setting fire to the forest. Even if we evade the dragon, we won't be able to evade the fire.

Passing the bunker, we keep running as fast as we can. We can't outrun a dragon. I know he can see us but I'm hoping the trees conceal us enough. Joffrey and I reach the end of the forest and come to a halt at the edge of a high cliff that drops into a deep ravine.

"Can we make this jump?" I ask.

There is no time to decide. The dragon is closing in on us. Taking a deep breath, I leap off the cliff. For a moment, I feel free. Flying above, like the dragon. Once I hit the water, I go into shock. Cold needles stab my legs, arms, stomach, everywhere. It's paralyzing. With everything I have, I force myself to swim. I surface and try to keep calm as my body violently trembles. Seconds later, Joffrey tops the water.

The iciness of the water hurts. My muscles ache, and I can feel my body tiring. I have to get out of this.

"We need to keep moving." He takes my hand and helps pull me to the side under a jutting rock where we are completely hidden from view.

My teeth chatter and ironically, I wish for fire.

Joffrey pulls me closer to him and rubs my arm. "This will keep us warm."

Clutching the bag of potions close to my chest, I realize that maybe we should've taken more people with us. But that would have only put more lives in danger. I've done enough of that.

"Are you okay?" Joffrey asks.

I nod, craving warmth.

His eyebrows draw together. "I can't build a fire. The dragon will see it."

As if on cue, a dark shadow glides above us. We tuck ourselves closer under the rock. My eyes train on the dragon as it searches for us. His screams echo in the ravine. Back and forth, it examines the area for us. The whole time I hold my breath, for fear it can hear. I hope it can't detect the pounding of my heart.

Finally, after what seems like hours, he flies away. Both of us breathe a sigh of relief.

"We have to get back," I say.

"The witch didn't put a healing potion in there, did she?"

I shake my head.

"Are you ready to start walking back?"

Not really. "Yes." When I get to my feet, exhaustion pours over me. I ignore it as we trek through the narrow path beside the ravine, hoping that we survive this.

We travel for hours and the only thing that keeps me going is seeing Casper. I can still hear the dragon miles away, screaming. It's a different kind of shriek that I've heard before. This cry sounds like it's sad. Maybe it is Vincent, and he thinks I'm dead. That only helps our case.

As we return to the cave, I can't help but feel nostalgic for the human world with Casper again. I'm not sure why my mind continues to return there, why I feel such a strong connection to it. Part of me wants to reach into my pocket, pull out my phone and text Cherry about the dragon. Ask Jonathan if he thinks I'm making the right decision.

I wonder what my family and Cherry think happened to me. Casper's family? His mom helped me that night after the party. I hate how we never got to say goodbye to them, but Casper and I will be able to make new memories once Vincent is dead. We'll all be able to live free. The thought gives me more strength as we slowly make our way back.

<h1 style="text-align:center">Thirty-Five</h1>

rey ash continues to fall from the night sky as we approach the cave. My legs ache and I know any second, I'm going to collapse. *Just a little further*. That's all Joffrey has said, especially once the sky darkened. The further from the ravine we got, the less we heard the dragon. We're both dehydrated, exhausted, and bordering delirium.

Once I see the opening of the cave, tears spring to my eyes.

"We're here." Joffrey almost carries me toward the entrance and the second Casper looks up, he darts toward us.

"Megan, are you hurt?"

"We're exhausted. We ran into trouble, we're okay now."

"Thank you for keeping her safe."

"Of course. She's the one who kept me safe." Joffrey heads toward the cave.

"Really?" Casper says and I'm a bit miffed that he seems surprised I could do that.

I shake my head as if to banish the thoughts.

Tangling myself in his arms, Casper kisses the top of my head. His breath tickles my hair.

"Megan." The way he says my name so gravely causes an ache in my stomach. I didn't know if I would see him again. Too many times I've felt that way. "You're here. You're okay."

I nod, unable to speak. Lifting me in his arms, he carries me into a corner inside the cave.

Cyran attends to both Joffrey and me. I chug as much water as I can. My headache is still there. I know it'll take some time to wear off.

Sitting up, Casper gathers me in his arms. "I missed you."

Florence approaches us and wraps her arms around me. "I'm so happy you're back. We were so worried about you."

I nod. "I'm sorry."

"Zev and I are heading out in the morning to put the plan in motion."

Nerves twist inside my stomach. "Just the two of you?"

"You know that's all who can come." She kneels beside me and puts a reassuring hand on my arm. "We'll be okay. The plan will work. Get some rest and I'll see you when it's over."

Her words bring some ounce of comfort, even though tears cloud my vision. "Please be safe."

Florence gives a small smile. "We will." She lifts my chin to force me to look at her. "No more tears. We will win this."

Casper holds me closer and kisses my temple. "Do you feel like sleeping?"

"Yes. I'm too scared of the nightmares."

"Want to talk about it?"

"A dragon found us."

He tenses and lets out a curse. "I wish more of us went."

"It would've put more people in danger. I wished I could've called you to let you know I was okay."

He chuckles. "This world is certainly different, isn't it?"

I nod. "We ran from the dragon and jumped into a freezing ravine. It was the only thing we could do."

"I'm so thankful you are safe and I'm proud of you. No more journeys without me. I can't handle not being there with you. You did great, Megan. You're back, safe and sound."

I feel a twinge of shame, knowing I prevented him from joining us. "It's okay." Tears spring to my eyes and I try so hard to push them away. I don't have much time with Casper before the plan is in place.

"Why were you okay with me staying here?"

I look up, meeting his eyes. "I wasn't. I wanted you there with me. I always want you with me. You know it's too dangerous right now. Something is always preventing us from being together."

"I know. Something feels like it's changed though. I know there's a lot going on right now, even when we're together, you seem sad or like you're somewhere else or like you want to be somewhere else."

I frown. "I'm sorry."

"What is it?"

I exhale. "I miss the human world. I know I have to give it up."

"Do you think you won't be happy here?"

"No. It's not that. I can't explain it. Once I return and say goodbye, I won't feel that way any longer."

"When you are able to return, will you tell my parents that I love them? They were the best parents I ever had."

"Of course."

He kisses me and I deepen the kiss, eager to share my life with him. Forever. Even though my heart feels like it's being ripped in half.

Thirty-Six

A gentle voice pulls me from a deep sleep. When I wake, I'm met with those beautiful brown eyes. A smile stretches across my face.

"Good afternoon," Casper says. He nuzzles in the crook of my neck, kissing me.

"I love waking up next to you. I know we haven't gotten to a lot; I plan to change that."

I smile once more as he kisses me. Even though we're in a private area of the cave, I don't want anyone walking up while we're in the middle of something.

Sitting up, Casper and I cuddle with each other.

"I miss sleeping in a bed."

He lets out a soft laugh. "You and me both."

For the next several days, Casper and I spend as much time as we can together, anxiously waiting for Florence and Zev to return. In that time with him, I only fell in more love with him. Loving how caring he is and his undivided attention.

But I hate what I've become to be with him. I hate that he feels he has to protect me all the time. Yes, I was attacked, but I can handle my own.

"What was your favorite memory of us from this past human life?" I ask him.

He mulls it over as we meander through the forest near the cave. We don't stray far from the cave, still close enough to return if needed. I hope Florence is okay and that nothing happens to her.

"Probably our first kiss. It was one of the most intense kisses I've ever had."

"Really?"

He smirks. "Always. What about you?"

"Honestly? All of it. If I had to choose, I loved getting to know you or the night of the attack. After it. I was a mess on the verge of falling apart, but you held me together. I knew then how much you cared about me."

"It took a while to convince you." He teases.

"I know." I softly laugh.

It seems surreal how calm everything is considering that we're on the verge of a war. I push it from my mind and relish this moment with him.

Deeper into the forest, we find ourselves on the beach. I long for a bath, or anything. I know we shouldn't.

"Come on," I say. "We won't be long."

He nods and follows me to the incredibly aqua water, the waves begging us to enter. We shed our clothes and jump in. The water is a little chilly, nowhere near as bad as the ravine. Casper grabs me, lifting me with the waves. When he lowers me, my mouth lands on his in an urgent manner. I wish it could always be like this. I know it can't but it's nice to wish. If only for tonight, we are two lovers on an abandoned island. There is no war. There is no pain. Only us.

After we play a little longer in the ocean, we dress and return to the cave. Commotion from inside alerts us and we pick up our pace. Once we reach the large room inside, I see everyone standing, then I see Florence.

She turns around to face me with tears in her eyes. Dread hits the pit of my stomach.

"What is it?" I ask.

"Th-they killed Zev."

I gasp.

Casper balls his hands into fists and his expression darkens. I hate how much our emotions change from one extreme to the next.

"Why?" I ask, feeling my temper rising. Why would they kill Zev? Did they not believe Florence?

"He tried to make it look like he was running after me, and they shot him."

"What did they say?" Casper asked through clenched teeth.

"Vincent agreed to meet with us in the meadows at sundown."

The meadows. That's where Joffrey and I left the horses. The dragon was Vincent. "Does he think I'm dead?"

"He says he saw you jump off a cliff and never resurface."

So that was Vincent. "Good."

"We've only a few hours," Cyran says, and my stomach clenches. I have to give Casper the sleeping potion. "Joffrey and I brought Ena's body. She is ready."

My mind races. Can I do this? Can I do this without Casper by my side? Saliva collects in my mouth, and I want to throw up. Anxiety itches beneath my chest and I'm shaking.

"Are you ready?" Cyran asks me.

I nod. "Yes. Let me get ready."

"Casper, can you help me with Ena's body?" Joffrey asks and I know he's trying to distract Casper while I get the syringe ready.

"Sure." He kisses me and follows Joffrey.

Clenching my fists and my teeth, I make my way to mine and Casper's little area of the cave. Grabbing the bag of potions, I kneel and take a deep breath. Everything is happening too fast. I try calming my breaths and I swallow the lump in my throat.

Silvyr seeks me out. "Are you okay to follow through?"

"Yes."

Digging for Casper's potion, I grab the syringe and fill it. I hold the serum in my shaky hand and push the nausea away. Wrapping the bag strap across my chest, I get to my feet.

My heart lurches to my chest as I see Casper walking toward me. I don't want him to be ready. I don't want to do this. Silvyr gives him a nod and walks away.

"Everything okay?"

I smile. "Yes. I think he has quite the crush on Florence."

He nods slowly. I know he doesn't believe me. "Are you okay, Megan? You're looking extremely pale."

"Yeah, no I'm fine." I inhale a deep breath.

"You're worried this won't work, aren't you? This will work."

"I know." Tears brim the surface of my eyes.

"It's going to be okay. I promise. We're going to get through this." His thumbs wipe away my tears. "No matter what, I will always be here. I will do whatever it takes to keep you safe." He presses his forehead against mine and pulls me closer. My heart jumps like always and I long for his kiss. He smells amazing and I inhale, almost as if trying to preserve it to my memory. The feel of his arms. The sound of his voice.

No matter what, I won't let us be apart, I need to do this without him. If Casper shows his face, they will kill him without hesitation. They'll know something is up. I remind myself.

Casper takes my face in between his hands and presses his warm lips to mine. His love gives me the strength I need. He always has. He has always loved me, no matter what. No matter who I am, or what I've done. He has always let me be free and let me be myself. He has always held me when I needed a cry.

He has always made me laugh and given me everything I've needed. This is why I must keep him safe. It's my turn to keep the man I love safe.

When he draws back, a bulge forms in my throat. I don't want to say goodbye, even if it may be temporarily. Tilting my head toward his face, I kiss him in an urgent manner and hold him closer. He tangles his hand in my hair, kissing me harder. I don't want this to end. I want to keep my eyes closed and live in the ecstasy of this moment and pretend that everything is peaceful like our human lives. I could hold him forever.

We can't do that. Reality isn't like that and sometimes you have to go through hell in order to live again.

Holding the syringe in my hand, I falter in my kiss. I bring my hand up and softly stab Casper in the neck, pushing the serum inside him.

He pulls away, his eyebrows wrinkle and I can't stop the tears. He grabs his neck. "What did you do?"

"I'm sorry. I had to."

"Megan?" He snatches the syringe from my hand. "What did you do?" His eyes darken and he slams the needle to the ground.

"You wouldn't have supported the idea. This ensures your safety."

"What did you do?"

I bite my lip. "It's a serum. To put you to sleep, long enough for us to carry out this plan and for you to be safe."

Casper shakes his head. "What are you talking about? You're just going to leave me here while you go? How could you do this?"

"Silvyr will keep you safe."

His face falls and his eyes are laden with anger. Gripping the back of his neck, he turns away. He lets out a frustrated moan. He faces me, fear crossing his eyes. "Megan, no—" He closes his eyes. He swallows hard, stumbling.

"Casper, please understand."

He struggles from the fast-working potion. It quickly overpowers him. He falls to his knees. I catch him and ease him to the ground.

"I'm so sorry, Casper. I had to."

"Why would you do this?" He snaps.

"Because Vincent would've killed you."

"You have no faith in me."

"No. That's not it."

"I can't believe you would do this. You think you're going to die, don't you? This...is this how you say goodbye to me?"

My stomach drops and I feel sick. Hearing him say that makes me doubt my decision and I feel the betrayal I've done. I hate what I've done but I have to continue with the plan. With everything I have, I will make it back to Casper.

"Casper, I will never say goodbye. I love you, but you deserve to be safe. You cannot die because of me. I will end this and come back to you. You have my word."

He slowly shakes his head and tries to grip my hand. I know it'll be seconds when the potion finally takes over completely. "I love you, Megan."

"I love you, Casper. Always."

"Don't do this. Please don't leave..."

His eyes close, and I inhale a shaky breath. It doesn't stop the tears. Watching him sleep reminds me of the time he was in the hospital. He looked so peaceful that time, as he does now. He is beautiful and I want to memorize the lines on his face, the way he looks at me, the way he smiles. I brush aside a lock of his blonde hair, lean down and kiss him on the lips.

"I promise I will be back for you. I love you," I whisper in his ear.

Silvyr and Cyran approach us, the closer they get, the more the pain in my heart grows.

"Everything will be okay," Cyran says. "He will be safe. Nothing will happen to him."

As they lift his body, the pain intensifies, and heaviness overcomes me. They carry his body further inside the cave, keeping him safe.

When he wakes, we will have killed Vincent.

Thirty-Seven

lorence rushes to my side as they take away Casper. I know he's not dead. It feels like I have lost the one person who understands me completely, who loves me unconditionally, who would do anything for me. When I can't see him any longer, the tears consume me. I have failed and disappointed him. He won't forgive me.

"It's going to be okay, Megan." Florence lifts my chin forcing me to meet her eyes. "We will come back. You will see him again."

I shake my head. "He won't forgive me."

A wrinkle appears between her eyebrows. "Of course, he will. He loves you like no one ever has. He'll be upset, yes but he will forgive you."

Joffrey places a hand on my shoulder. "We will defeat the Sprites."

As Florence lifts the vial with the semivivus, my heart lurches to my chest. "It's time," she says.

"Not yet." I'm not ready. I want more time with Casper. More time with Florence. More time.

But she's right.

She frowns. "This will stop the pain until you wake. When you do, I will be right beside you and we can kill Vincent together."

Taking the potion from her, I breathe in a shaky breath. Placing the serum to my lips, I close my eyes, pausing.

Then, I drink.

The army waits for us on the edge of the forest, ready to attack. It will take us exactly thirty-five minutes for us to reach our meeting point. I have one shot. One shot to kill Vincent.

My eyes are heavy, and I want to lie down. Not from the potion. My heart weighs me down. Florence lets me lean against her shoulder. She strokes my hair, calming me. I close my eyes and feel the potion work its way through my veins. My breathing slows.

"Just rest. Everything will be fine. Our revenge will work. It's always amazed me how trusting you are. You all have fallen into our wonderful trap. You know, you will never kill Vincent."

Sifting through the fog in my mind, I force my eyes open. "What?"

"You won't even get close to him." A sinister grin spreads across her face.

"What are you talking about?" Drawing back from her, I fight against the heavy potion. I can barely lift a muscle.

"You really should've listened to Ena, but you didn't."

"About what?" What is she saying? Where is Joffrey? The faster my heart beats, the faster I can feel the potion work itself.

"About who you can trust."

"Wh-what did you do?"

"What had to be done."

I'm trying my best to remember what Ena said about Florence. *She sold you out. She told the Sprites where you and Casper ran away.* "You...you told Vincent."

"Ahh. You *do* remember what she said. You were right about one thing: he will make a great king."

I can feel the blood draining from my face. What has she done? "Vincent killed Edmond."

"He did and I escaped. I found you and Casper that night at the witch's cabin. I sent a note to Vincent letting him know what you had done. The Elves captured me and held me captive after that. For my life and freedom, I told Vincent the truth. He needed to know."

A sickening feeling settles in my stomach. "You...sold me out? You were my friend."

She lets out a dry laugh. "You never cared about me. You only cared about yourself and Casper."

"Why are you doing this?" My voice is weak, the words jumbling together.

"Because you took enough from me. You left me to die and gave up on me. You never even came to look for me. You assumed I was dead. You never cared about what I wanted. Ever since Casper came into your life, he possessed you. You gave up everything for him. Now you'll know what it's like to have everything give up on you. To lose everything."

"Florence, no."

"I hoped Vincent would've killed you both. No such luck. He'll be so proud of me. Too bad you won't get to see us arrest Casper and slice his head from his body for all the Sprites to see."

I want to strangle her. Tear her heart out. I can't breathe. I can't move. The potion is consuming me. This isn't real. I'm dreaming. The serum is working much faster than I thought it would. It's such a struggle. My energy is depleting. I'm having a difficult time staying upright or even keep my eyes open.

My throat is dry. I start to crawl away from her. I don't get far.

A figure moves into the cave and once they are close enough, I gasp. The Nuummite Jewel reflects off a light. He holds up a head by its blonde hair. For a second, I think it's Casper but when I see Joffrey's face, my insides twist.

"No!"

"Hello, Megan." Vincent tosses Joffrey's head to the ground and makes his way toward me.

A flush of adrenaline tingles throughout me and my heartbeat races. My cheeks burn and I know I've been defeated. I shake my head and turn to Florence. "What is this? You brought him *here*?"

"I did. The Sprites will annihilate the Elves. Did you think I was on your side? After everything you've done. After you betrayed us so many times for these *Elves*. I am a Sprite; I will always be one."

The serum moves through my veins, weakening me even more. My body feels as if it's cemented to the ground. I need to get away from both of them. How can Florence do this to me? To us? The Queen was right about her all along. I trusted Florence. She had been my friend for centuries.

"How could you plot my death?" Vincent asks, pain flashing in his dark blue eyes. "You were never going to die that day at the gallows. I had a plan to save you. But like always, you chose to believe I am the bad guy. Then those vile creatures killed many of us to save you. Always you. Yet, I realize you only care for yourself. For someone who doesn't deserve your attention."

"That's not true."

"You know what you have to do to save yourself. If you let him go, Megan, all of this will end."

"No!"

"Stop being selfish!" Florence says. "You see nothing but him. You don't know what you've done."

Vincent holds up his hand to her and kneels next to me. He sweeps a few strands of hair from my face. His touch is cold. "You've betrayed all of us because of him. Finding out you were going to kill me." He shakes his head. "You disappointed me. You hurt me. You never loved me. I never would've killed you. I never will." He breathes in a deep breath. "Now, I will ask you once more. Will you give him up completely in order to live?"

I glare at him. "I would rather die a thousand deaths than be with you."

His eyes turn cold and emotionless. He smirks. "So be it." Vincent holds the Jewel and grabs my hand.

I try to pull back, but I can't overpower him. "What are you doing?"

"Taking you back where you belong."

I shake my head. I can't go back to Château de Fées and live my life in a cell. I can't do it. I can't fight against him. "No, please."

"You can't let him go. This is the only way."

The grey vortex wraps around us, wind and loud sounds surrounds us, stealing us away. I force myself to stay awake, to try to fight.

When the vortex stops, everything is silent. I look around but it's too dark. I see lights coming toward us from a distance. Two of them.

"Where," is all I can muster to say. I want to get out of his disgusting grip. I want to kill him but I'm much too weak. How did I not see this?

"You are where you belong. You will live each human life wishing for something that will never exist for you. You will have no way to return, and Casper won't be alive to save you. Your dreams will remain silent in each lifetime."

He brought me back to the human world? "No. Please."

"I hope it was worth it. You could've been Queen and have all the riches in the world. You chose to forsake your own kind and now, you have nothing."

"That isn't true. I will have my freedom from you."

He takes my face between his hands, and I know he's going to wipe my memories. I try to fight him with my mind, the serum made me too weak.

"Megan, this is for your own good. Since you refuse to give Casper up, I have no choice but to do this."

"No, please. I'll do whatever you want. Please don't kill him."

"He's already dead. You need to face that reality."

"No."

"I will not erase your memories, but no one will speak his name, and no one will believe your story, no matter how hard you try to convince them. But you *will* remember me."

"Don't do this."

"Until you are fully ready to move on from him, this has to be done. Farewell, mon trésor."

A loud crack sounds. Vincent vanishes. I feel myself floating in the air, if just for a moment. My back. The pain intensifies. Frantic voices surround me. None of them are Vincent or Casper. Vincent has left me here. He will kill Casper. I must fight through this. I must save Casper.

The voices are fading. I close my eyes. There is nothing but blackness. There are no sounds.

There is nothing.

Thirty-Eight

ights blind me when I open my eyes, the brightness sears into me. I shield the intensity. Blinking several times, my vision becomes sharp. To my right is an IV stand. Liquid slowly drips down into a tube. I follow it to the vein on my hand. There's a light above me but it's dim. I'm in a hospital bed, hooked up to several machines. Everything is modern. Am I in the human world? I have to be.

I can barely keep my eyes open. It feels like I haven't slept for days.

I can't remember why I'm in the hospital or how I got here.

Then it all comes back. Vincent. The vortex. Florence selling me out. Me putting Casper to sleep and Vincent threatening to kill him.

Pain shoots through me and I cry out. A searing ache throbs in my lower back and it feels like there's a tight band around my head, squeezing it causing an unrelenting throb.

The door opens and a nurse runs inside. "Megan? You're awake." She pushes a button and slowly, the pain begins to subside.

"Where?" I speak, my mouth is incredibly dry. I'm so drowsy and thirsty.

"It's okay. Here." She brings a cup with a straw to my mouth. "Drink."

I take a sip of the lukewarm water. "Where am I?"

She frowns. "You're in the hospital, dear. Do you remember what happened?"

I shake my head. Did Vincent put me in here? What happened before he vanished? The more I try to remember, the more my head pounds.

"It's okay. I'm going to get the doctor."

A few minutes later, a tall balding man enters. "Megan, I'm Dr. Ellis. Do you remember what happened?"

"Vincent...he brought me back. He vanished."

"It's okay." He checks my pulse. Flashes a light in both my eyes.

I'm so groggy and disoriented. I want to sleep but I also want to get out of here. "Why am I in the hospital?"

Dr. Ellis frowns. "You were shot, dear."

Shot? Vincent shot me again?

I can't stand this feeling. I want to get up and move around and talk but it's like I'm paralyzed. I can barely make out any words. The witch could've warned about the intense disorientation from the potion. Though I should have known given that it was something that made me appear dead. "I'm in so much pain. My back."

"I know. I upped the morphine. I've called your parents. They're on their way. Get some rest for now."

"Vincent brought me back here, said I deserved to be here. I have to get back to Casper." I can barely keep my eyes open.

Dr. Ellis gives a confused look, then pats my arm. "Your memories will be a bit messy for a while, but I think they'll return."

"Why are you looking at me like I'm crazy?" I slur through my words.

"Megan, it's best if you rest and not worry right now. You've been through a lot."

The morphine is kicking in, but I want to know why he's looking at me that way. "Please, what's the matter?"

Dr. Ellis frowns. "You've woken up from a coma. You were shot but everything is okay now."

Now it's my turn to look at him like he's lost his marbles. *Coma*? I shake my head, feeling sleepier. "How long have I been here?"

"A little over a month. Get some rest, Megan."

A month? What is going on? Did the witch's potion put me in a coma? Did Vincent? How could he do this? What did he do? I can't believe he left me here. How am I going to return?

Casper. I left him and I know Vincent and Florence are going to kill him. I have to get out of here.

I have to get back. I have to figure out a way. Maybe the witch can see what happened and find me or I can find her.

"I have to go." I make a lousy attempt at lifting the blanket from me.

Dr. Ellis stops me. "Please, Megan, rest."

I have to save Casper before it's too late. I know Vincent wouldn't kill him when he's still asleep. He'll torture him first. Now that he has him all to himself. I have to believe that. I have to believe that Casper is still alive, and I will save him.

"I have to save him."

"It's okay. You're safe." He pushes a button and calls for a nurse to bring him something.

She enters with a syringe.

"She's a bit anxious," Dr. Ellis tells the nurse.

"Hi sweetie," she says. "It's okay. I'm going to add a little medicine to help with the anxiety."

A tear falls down my cheek. "I have to save him."

Both the doctor and nurse frown before I shut my eyes.

I must search for Casper in my dreams. He must be there. We've always found each other that way. It's the only way to reach him. I have to warn him. It's the only way to be with him until we are together again.

PLAYLIST

Evanescence – Lost in Paradise (Synthesia version)
The Birthday Massacre –Under Your Spell
The Boxer Rebellion – Promises
Jimmy Eat World – Disintegration
Ruelle – I Get to Love You
Florence + The Machine – Stand By Me
Indiana – Bound
Sleeping Wolf – The Wreck of Our Hearts
Tegan and Sara – I Was a Fool
Tori Amos – Carry
Dawn Richard & Mumdance – Guardian Angel
Cloves – Don't Forget About Me
X Ambassadors – Unsteady (Erich Lee Gravity Remix)
Evanescence – Bring Me to Life (Synthesia version)
Hidden Citizens – Here We Stand
Of Monsters and Men – Thousand Eyes
Chord Overstreet – Hold On

Carrigan Richards is the young adult author of critically acclaimed *Pieces of Me*, a contemporary romance, the *Elemental Enchanters Series*, a paranormal romance series, and *January Dreams Series*, a romantic mystery series. She lives in Atlanta, Georgia.

When she's not writing (which is rare), she's spending time with her family and friends, listening to music, playing with her furbaby, Eli, or cheering on her Atlanta Braves. Carrigan loves hearing from readers. Social: @authorcarriganrichards

www.carriganrichards.com